THE SWAN KINGDOM

Zoë Marriott is twenty-four years old and says she has been waiting to write *The Swan Kingdom*, her debut novel, since she was a child. "When I was six, my sister brought me an illustrated picture book version of Hans Christian Andersen's *The Wild Swans*. The story immediately captured my imagination and has stayed with me ever since." Zoë works as a civil servant and in her spare time likes to paint, hike and read. She lives in north-east Lincolnshire and has two cats named Echo and Hero.

*This book is dedicated to
ugly ducklings everywhere.*

*Don't worry about those fluffy
yellow morons: they'll never get
to be swans.*

First published 2007 by Walker Books Ltd
87 Vauxhall Walk, London SE11 5HJ

2 4 6 8 10 9 7 5 3

Text © 2007 Zoë Marriott
Cover illustration © 2007 Steve Rawlings

This book has been typeset in Golden Cockerel

Printed in Great Britain by Cox & Wyman Ltd, Reading, Berkshire

British Library Cataloguing in Publication Data:
a catalogue record for this book
is available from the British Library

ISBN 978-0-7445-2927-2

www.walkerbooks.co.uk

The Swan Kingdom

ZOË MARRIOTT

WALKER BOOKS
AND SUBSIDIARIES
LONDON · BOSTON · SYDNEY · AUCKLAND

PART ONE

PROLOGUE

My first memory is of the smell of sun-warmed earth.

I must have been very small, perhaps only two or three years old. I remember my mother's hands, stubby-fingered and calloused, covered with soil as she gently eased a plant from the ground. She talked quietly to me as she worked, explaining that the plant lived by spreading roots through the earth, taking moisture and nourishment from the land, and using the warmth of the sun to grow strong. She told me the name of the herb she tended – lady's hook – and its uses in cooking and medicine, and described how it might be dried or steeped in oil. And then, when the plant had been carefully potted, she cupped a handful of the rich dark soil and showed me its power.

Before my wondering eyes, each tiny particle sprang

to life, shining and beautiful, awash with eddying power. Astonished, I lifted my eyes to look at my mother's garden. I could see the same beauty in all the plants and in the trees that ringed us. The clouds above us were alive too – the current of life even swirled in the air.

When my newly awakened eyes returned to my mother, she was suffused with the intense glow – my eyes were filled with the brightness of her. Power flowed through her body, coursing in her veins like blood. She leaned towards me, taking my tiny hands in her dirt-caked fingers.

"It is the enaid, Alexandra." She whispered. "The life of the world. It is in the earth, in the waters, the animals and the green things. It is in the air. And we – you and I – are its heart. As long as we are here to care for this land, nothing can change that."

I remember how her words seemed to resound within me, as if something inside my heart had stirred and mumured my name. And when I looked down at my hands, clasped in hers, I saw that same rush of power shining in my own veins.

CHAPTER
ONE

You probably know me already. In every story you've ever been told, someone like me exists. A figure in the background, barely noticed by the main players. A talentless, unwanted child. The ugly one. The ugly one only ever gets in the way. She is as out of place as a sparrow in a clutch of swans. This was the role I had in my father's Hall.

It was the role my father gave me.

I have a memory. It's smudgy, almost faded into nothing now. It's a memory of my father. I can remember him picking me up in his big arms and whirling me around until I shrieked with laughter. I can remember him calling me his sweeting. But that's the last – the only – time I can ever remember him holding me.

I don't know what changed. Maybe it was me. I was

not like my brothers – whom, it must be said, he did love a great deal. I must have been a great disappointment as a King's daughter. I could not be married off to his advantage, for who would want to wed a creature so plain? And I was a strange little girl, always talking to things other people couldn't see, running off on my own, never listening to his orders. I can understand why he might have despaired of me. I don't understand why he stopped loving me.

But I adapted, in the way that children do. For I held another place in my father's Hall – the place my mother and brothers gave me.

It's not enough to say that my mother was beautiful, though she was, almost unbelievably so. But her beauty was the least that people said of her. She was a wise woman, renowned throughout the Kingdom. That was why my father, the king, had wed her. In truth, her compassion and gentleness made her better loved than father, with his harsh ideas of justice and his brusque manner, could ever have been. Everyone adored her. I idolized her.

And then there were my brothers. I loved them almost as dearly as I did my mother.

David was the eldest, my father's heir and the most like him, with his dark hair and eyes. He was calm and steady, and it was he who endeavoured to keep my dresses unmuddied and the twigs from my hair.

Next came Hugh, the tallest and most handsome,

with golden hair and the careless, flashing smile of our mother. He was quick and witty and could tease even our father from a black mood. He was the inventor – and victor – of all our childhood games.

Robin was the closest to me in age as well as temperament. He was not a brilliant swordsman like David or a fine horseman like Hugh. He was a thinker, and kept his nose in a book as often as he could manage; but for me he always had time – to talk, paint pictures, play games. When I found the sparrow with a broken wing, it was Robin I ran to, and he put aside his book and showed me how to splint its bone and feed it, his hands and voice gentle. Robin and I were alike in many ways. We had the same deep auburn-coloured hair. We had both inherited Mother's eyes, the vivid green of newly unfurled leaves.

But there, I'm afraid, my resemblance to Robin or my mother ended.

When I said I was ugly, I meant it. Though I had my mother's hair and eyes and her pale skin, somehow I was ... ugly. Or perhaps that's too strong a word. It was just that my small, white face, with its delicate features, faded into insignificance, especially next to the dazzling charms of the rest of my family. They said David would make a wonderful king, in time. There was no doubt that Hugh would be a fine lord, and defend his brother's lands well. And Robin, of course, would be a great scholar.

No one said what I would become. They looked at me with pity, I think. I was nothing. I was the wanderer, the dreamer who listened to the tides of magic in her sleep. I knew it was not my destiny to be great. I would only be Alexandra, and I would be free.

So I wasn't unhappy, then. The wood-frame Hall, with its curved walls and thatching that almost reached the ground in places, was a true home to me, and I loved it, especially Mother's beautiful gardens that spread out over most of the hillside. I grew up running wild through the amber fields of the Kingdom, sleeping in the green and silver shadows of its forests, diving through the clear sweetness of its waters. My brothers ran with me, and my mother watched over us all. When I look back now, my memories of that time seem to stream and dance like dust motes gilded by the sun.

I remember one afternoon in late summer when I was about ten. Robin and I lay next to each other in the grasses by the hawthorn hedge, watching the clouds wheel above us in the sky. The hump of thatching that was the roof of the Hall was just out of sight over the curve of the hill, and below us was wild land dotted with daisies, forget-me-nots and ammemnon flowers.

Hugh and David had found some long sticks and were mock duelling near by. Their shouts and swearing didn't disturb me – I was far too used to it – but Hugh's yelp of pain at David's blow to his knuckles was particularly loud, and I rolled my eyes at Robin as Hugh proceeded to curse his opponent soundly.

"How can David's father have been a mongrel cur with one leg?" I called lazily. "He's your father too."

"I refuse to believe it," Hugh said dramatically. "Obviously David is the goblin child that Mother found by the wayside one day and took pity on."

"Unlikely," David said, lowering his stick. He leaned on it, continuing thoughtfully, "But it might be true that one of us is a changeling."

I blinked in shock, and sat up. "Do you mean me?" I asked, my voice sounding too high-pitched even to my own ears.

"Don't be stupid," Hugh said hastily. "You're the living spit of Mother."

"I mean Hugh, of course." David agreed calmly. "You and Robin both look like mother, and I obviously take after Father. But who does Hugh look like?"

"Oh," I said, relieved. "Mama says he looks like her sister."

"Hmm. Possibly. But if Hugh is a goblin child it would explain his abominable sword work," David said.

"Pah!" Hugh raised the stick in his hand threateningly. "Say that to my sword, coward."

"Oh, no more, please." Robin finally spoke, rolling over. "You're too noisy. Come and watch clouds, or else go and fight in the stable yard."

"Too noisy?" cried Hugh dramatically. He flung his stick into the hedge, startling a pair of blackbirds into flight. "I'll teach you to cheek your elders, worm!"

Robin looked at Hugh in alarm, scrambling to his feet, but Hugh grabbed him and easily wrestled him back to the ground.

"Help!" Robin shouted, the word muffled by Hugh's arm. "Alex!"

I threw myself onto Hugh's back and began tickling him mercilessly, knowing this was his greatest weakness. He immediately convulsed with uncontrollable laughter, forced to release Robin as he tried to swat me away.

"Treachery!" he shouted between gales of laughter. "Betrayal – ow!"

Robin wormed out from under us and sat on Hugh's legs. "Surrender!"

"Never. I'll die first!" Hugh squirmed helplessly under our combined weight. Weak with laughter myself now, I almost fell off, and laughed all the harder.

David watched us wonderingly. "Well, I think that settles it," he said. "I must be the changeling, since I refuse to admit I'm related to any of you."

Hugh, Robin and I froze, and turned to look at David. Then Robin shouted, "Get him!"

David dropped his stick and ran, and the three of them jumped up and chased after him, laughing like loons.

But as much fun as I had with my brothers, the brightest point of any day was that spent with my mother, in her gardens. Before I was old enough even to talk, my mother had given me lessons in her gardens each morning – lessons I took much more seriously than the sporadic lectures I received from the household women on embroidery or how a lady should curtsy.

In Mother's gardens, all things were named, and all named things were beautiful, from the tiny, glistening beetles that crawled under the rocks, to the magnificent fragrant roses, to the birds that streamed by overhead. Mother taught me about everything important in the world, about the plants and trees, animals and feathered things, about the weather, about how to care for the land and make it fertile. She taught me of the countries to the west, where the rulers loved music so much that they spent every crumb of gold on harpists and singers, while their people starved to death. She taught me of the nation to the north, where ambitious men had ripped the land apart with civil wars until roses would no longer bloom in the place they had once called the City of Flowers. Only here, in the Kingdom, she said, were peace and plenty known. Only here were the Old Ways truly followed – the land respected and loved, and the Ancestors remembered and worshipped as they should be.

I soaked up her words as parched earth does the first

rains of spring, always thirsty for more. By the time I was ten I knew more plant lore than many herb women five times my age – could identify and name the uses of every plant in the gardens and the woods, knew all the draughts, poultices and potions that my mother could teach. I even added one or two new recipes to the huge, heavy tome of handmade paper that Mother laughingly called her spell book.

When I was eleven she began to teach me other things – what she called small workings. The small workings were just that: workaday things, little tricks for everyday life. I learned how to invite warmth into wood, so that kindling and tinderbox became unnecessary; to find the tiny flicker of life in even the most shrivelled of plants and coax it forth so that it might bloom again. I also learned how to call to living creatures with my thoughts and interpret the jumbled mix of images, smells and sensations that made up their language.

The power to do all this came from the earth, from the currents of life – called enaid – that ebbed and flowed across the land. Like many people, I had the ability to use this ambient power and draw strength from it. There were other women in the household and the surrounding villages who could do the same. Mother called them "cunning women" but not disparagingly. The folk of the Kingdom needed the women who could do these small things, for Mother could not be everywhere.

Mother, you see, had a different gift – a blessing from the Ancestors that allowed her to perform Great workings. The gift was one of healing, and it came from within her own body, not from the land. Mother could make people well whom any cunning woman would have given up for dead. When every poultice, potion and draught had failed, Lady Branwen could succeed. People came from all over the Kingdom and sometimes beyond, to seek her help; and she always gave it. She said that that was the price of the gift; that it must always be used. She also said that once there had been many women who had such power.

Now there was only her.

Mother never made me feel that I was a disappointment to her. In fact, sometimes I wondered if she was relieved that I had not inherited her gift. I knew such Great powers could be a burden, as well as a blessing. I had seen Mother grey and shaking with exhaustion after expending almost all her strength to save a life; and I had seen her weep bitterly when the gift was not enough to do so. Perhaps she was glad I had been spared such suffering. I could do small workings well enough; in some of them my skill even surpassed hers. With my knowledge of herbs and plants, of poultices and fomentations, I could offer comfort and the hope of recovery. But with that I had to be content. I had no Great gift.

My brothers thought my skills very useful. I could be asked to soothe a fractious horse, quickly warm a cold room in the Hall or hide the evidence of their picking fruit from Mother's gardens without permission. But when Hugh asked me to summon a deer to be shot, I grew so upset that Robin and David made him promise never to speak of it again.

My father did not find the turn my lessons had taken nearly so agreeable. After having heard the thoughts and feelings of animals — for, make no mistake, they have thoughts and feelings just as we do — I could no longer bear to eat meat. My mother had never done so, but to have his own daughter rebel in such a way was a great annoyance to Father. He was used to his people greeting the return of the Hunt with joyful faces and much anticipatory licking of lips, not tearful reproaches at the sight of the poor deer or boar slung over the rump of the horse. The first evening that I pushed my meat-filled trencher away was the first time I saw him argue with my mother.

That night the atmosphere in the long room was heavy and oppressive, as if thunderclouds lurked under the rafters, waiting to burst. The household people, wary of my father's mood, cleared away the remnants of the meal and hastily departed, and my brothers and I were dismissed from the room with a curt gesture from Father's hand. But I did not go. Disobeying his orders yet again, I hid behind one of the tapestries, and from my hiding place watched their fight in a churning of guilt and terror.

"How will I find a husband for her if she refuses to welcome the hunt, Branwen? It will be hard enough, homely as she is; but if she is seen to be simple-minded as well, no one will ever want her." He paced before the great stone mantel, his heavy boots thudding dully against the flagstones. "Is the satisfaction of defying me worth harming your own child? Because, make no mistake, you are harming her by insisting on this nonsense."

My mother sat dangerously still in her chair, hands clenched into stubby freckled fists on the tabletop as she faced him; but her voice was calm when she spoke.

"What nonsense do you speak of, My Lord? The teachings of the Ancestors? My teachings? That nonsense has kept this land fertile and rich for centuries. It has saved your blighted crops, healed your ailing animals, calmed the floods and bade the sun to smile on you. Is that the *nonsense* you mean?"

His face reddened in sudden rage and he slammed a hand on the mantel, making the whole hearth shake. "*I* rule this land. *I* am its master. The Old Ways are dead. The Ancestors smile on me because of the strength of my sword arm, not because of spells chanted by a witch woman!"

I gasped silently in my hiding place. Mama flinched as though he had struck her and swiftly turned her face away; I saw Father blanch as he realized the effect of his words.

It was then that I crept from behind the tapestry and into the gardens. I climbed up onto one of the low branches of the giant oak and laid my face against its bark, letting the whispering of the leaves soothe away the echo of the angry words and lull me to sleep.

The next morning, my mother looked sad and tired. I did not tell her what I had heard.

From then on our lessons were no longer the open and joyful times they had been. I was not even allowed to tell my brothers of what I learned, and I knew this was to keep the truth from my father. In the years that followed, I heard my parents argue only a handful of times, but I was observant enough to understand that harsh words were often exchanged behind the heavy doors of their bedchamber.

Time passed and my learning advanced. Gradually, through my mother's disparate lessons, I began to see a pattern in the world. The tides of enaid washed across the world, ever moving, unceasing and unsleeping. They bubbled up to allow growth and birth, and ebbed when there was death. And, gradually, I realized that there must be a source, a centre, the place where the enaid welled up into the land. My mother's teachings were leading me closer and closer to the knowledge of what that centre was, closer to understanding the place from which all the tides of life flowed. But when I asked about it, she pretended not to hear, and continued to teach me carefully, methodically, of the currents and moods of the tides, allowing me only glimpses of that great power which lay beyond. I wondered if it might be something entirely beyond my comprehension, and that was why she kept it from me. The thought hurt. Still, I had my family and my home, and my daily lessons continued.

I had no idea of the darkness that was about to befall us.

CHAPTER
TWO

The last normal day of my childhood was my fifteenth birthday. It was a day of great importance. Fifteen was when girls in the Kingdom were considered of an age to marry, and consequently a day for celebration in most girls' lives.

It was not quite the same for me. My father had no hope of marrying me off to advantage, for I was still lanky and plain, with a figure like a runner bean; and what was more, I was still wild and unheeding, still listened to my mother's words and ignored my father's, and talked to animals instead of eating them. I also had such a wealth of wisdom by that time that many a lord would have married me anyway, putting up with my homely face for the sake of my skills. But Father's indictment of my mother's lessons meant he had only the vaguest idea of my knowledge, and because he never troubled himself with what he called "women's gossip" he didn't know my name was held in high regard as a cunning woman. He had given up hope that I would ever bloom into a daughter he could be proud of.

Regardless of that, there was to be a banquet in my honour. It was tradition, after all; and my father was not, in general, a cruel man. So the evening of my fifteenth birthday a great fire was lit outside the Hall, fuelled with offerings of scented wood that would burn all night in thanks to the Ancestors. Lords and ladies from all the surrounding areas gathered in the long room to stuff themselves in my name. Because it was my feast, I was allowed to request all my favourite songs of the harpist and singer come to entertain us that night. I was even asked to dance a few times, by my brothers, of course, but also by some of the shy boys spurned by prettier girls.

When midnight came, I asked for one last song – my favourite. It was an ancient ballad called "The Tears of Mairid Westfield", which told the story of the doomed love of a peasant healer and a king. The king's jealous brother cast a spell over the healer and turned her into a grey fox, and the king, not knowing who the creature was when he found it in his rooms, drove his love away into the forest. The chorus had a haunting melody, and everyone always sang along with it:

"*The tears of Mairid Westfield*
Were her sorrowful goodbye;

The tears of Mairid Westfield
Could have drowned the starry sky.
For though she gave the warning,
Her love returned too late;
And the tears of Mairid Westfield
Could not change her woeful fate."

As I looked up from singing the last chorus, I realised that Father had gone. His chair at the head of our table was empty. In fact, I couldn't remember the last time I had seen him in the long room. My gaze turned to my mother, who tilted her head and gave me an apologetic look. I sighed.

I woke early the next morning and lay in my sunken bed, the carved wooden pillars rising above me. I stared, in that fixed, almost-awake way, at the intricate braiding of the thatched roof above me as I slowly became aware of the ache in my lower abdomen. I shifted uncomfortably, then frowned and lifted the quilted cover to stare down at the sticky brown stain on the inside of my thighs. With an odd mixture of apprehension and excitement I realized that I really was a woman now. My bleeding had begun.

I used the soft cloths my mother had given me the year before to bind myself, and then reached down into the earth, feeling for the ripples of enaid that told me where I would find her. I followed the movement of the tide, unsurprised to locate her in the gardens.

She was sitting on the grass, as she often did, in the shade of the dog rose that rambled over the southern wall of the Hall. Climbing plants were deadly to wood-frame buildings like the Hall – its wattle and daub walls and thatching could be pulled down by nothing more than ivy, if left unchecked. Mother was vigilant in making sure that no parasitic plants attached themselves to the building, but roses were her favourite and so she allowed this one limited freedom.

As soon as I saw her face, I knew there was no need to speak; she must have felt the resonance of my tangled emotions before I even stepped into the gardens. She patted the ground beside her, inviting me to sit.

"So, my darling," she said, her smile excited and girlish as she reached out to embrace me, "now you really are a woman. This is an important day for you. For us all."

She released me and absently began to prune the roses, and as she turned I thought I saw a different emotion flicker across her face. It might have been sadness; it might have been fear. I tried to understand the expression, but it was gone almost before I had seen it, and then I wondered if I had seen anything at all.

Her hardened fingers pinched the whippy stems deftly and the fibrous plant parted under her touch as easily as if she had applied shears. It was one of the first skills she had taught me, and since by now the gardens wore as almost as much mine as hers, I joined her. Our hands, working side by side, looked identical.

"In my great-grandmother's day, we would have had a celebration. A real celebration, nothing like that ... *civilized* thing last night. All the women of child-bearing age would have danced and sung to wild music in the Circle of Ancestors." She sighed and turned to me, a blowsy rose drooping in one hand. She swiftly stripped off the thorns, then leaned forward and tucked it carefully behind my ear in the thick mass of dark red hair.

"Circle of Ancestors?" I asked. I'd never heard her mention the name before.

"Ah. Never mind. In any case, I'm afraid we cannot do that today. Can you imagine the look on your father's face? But you and I must still mark the change in your life, Alexandra."

"How? What will we do?" I asked curiously.

"That's a surprise. I will come for you tonight, after everyone else has gone to bed, and then you will see."

She smiled mischievously, but I still thought she looked a little sad, so I nodded and did not press her. She reached out to touch my cheek with one rough finger as the smile died from her face. "You're strong," she whispered, more to herself than me. "Stronger than I am. You'll be all right."

The stillness of the moment was shattered by a harsh croak from above us. We both jumped and looked up to see a hooded crow peering at us from the thatching. It croaked again, rather smugly, I thought, and then took flight, casting a shadow over us as it went. It landed on the highest branch of the old oak and settled to watch us once more.

I pressed my hand against my thudding heart, feeling ridiculous for having jolted like a frightened rabbit. "Stupid creature," I muttered.

Mother laughed at my aggrieved tone, throwing back her head so that the sun seemed to spill through her hair like molten copper. "Perhaps he's a clever bird, and bored of our conversation," she said. "Let's give him something more exciting to watch. Dance, Alexandra!"

She jumped up, pulling me to my feet, and swirled me around as she had when I was a baby, her slender arms easily lifting me off the ground, though I was taller than she. Then she tripped over a spade, almost sending us both sprawling, and started laughing again at her own clumsiness. No one could listen to my mother laugh without joining in, so I laughed too, and the pair of us danced around the gardens, giggling madly for no reason, until we finally collapsed on the springy flock moss, gasping for breath.

The sun was only an hour set when I lay down among the knitted blankets and furs of my bed, stiff with nervous excitement. Outside, I could hear the gardens settling. An owl – Tawny by the sound of it – hooted gently from the tree by my window. The pinkish light faded with excruciating slowness, but there was no danger I might fall asleep. I was too excited, too apprehensive.

I felt the subdued echo of Mama's presence moments before she leaned through my open window, a finger at her lips. I got up, pulled on a fresh gown and went to her.

"Put this on," she whispered, passing me a bundle of fabric. I unfolded it to reveal a long cloak with a deep hood. It was a dull dark green colour, but the soft lining was holly-berry red. I clasped it at my throat, and then clambered over the sill to stand beside her in the darkness under the thatching, crushing the fragrant lavender under my feet. I accepted a small pack from her and slung it over my shoulder, then followed her out of the gardens and into the waving grasses of the meadow beyond.

"Where are we going?" I asked as soon as we were out of earshot of the Hall.

Mother lifted her face to the newly emerged stars, drawing in a deep breath before she answered. "You'll see."

There was a new tone in her voice, something I had never heard before. In the shadows of the night her whole aspect seemed changed, as if she were suddenly more than she had been while hemmed in by the walls of my father's Hall. Here she was not my father's lady, whom he liked to sit meekly at his side, but a queen in her own right – a ruler of kingdoms I had never seen. Her eyes glinted as they met mine and she smiled a secret smile. Together we walked down the hillside into the forest that began behind the Hall. I knew these woods well but they too seemed changed tonight, hushed and still.

At first the frosty light of the moon and stars filtered through the leaves and aided our passage, but as we went deeper into those ancient woods the trees grew older and taller, their canopies spreading immense mantles of shadow until only the vaguest glimmer of light could penetrate. Their trunks were thicker than the reach of my arms and grew so closely together that sometimes I had to turn sideways to slide between them. Mother ignored the deer tracks and paths worn by travellers and instead sought a different way that she seemed to know by instinct alone, for surely there was no landmark to guide her. If I had not been gifted with a cat's vision I should have come to a dozen accidents in the moist darkness. As it was, I tripped and stumbled along in her graceful wake, cursing in my mind at my own clumsiness. It was a warm spring that year, but here, where sunlight might never fall on the brightest day of summer, the darkness was chill, and before long I found myself shivering in the thin cloak Mama had given me. My increasing nervousness did not help. I had explored these woods a hundred, hundred times, sometimes alone, sometimes with my brothers – and yet I had never seen this place before. I had no idea where we were.

Eventually we broke from the towering darkness of the old trees into a clearing. It too, was strange to me, despite all my explorations; but suddenly I knew how

Mother had found her way. This place was powerful. Its presence sent out ripples into the enaid around it, which my nerves had stopped me sensingbefore. Now I was this close, it was like standing next to a waterfall.

At the centre of the circle of trees was an earthmound, perhaps as high as my shoulder. It was split by a slender opening that was supported on either side by two vertical slabs of rock, reaching up to a massive oval lintel stone embedded into the top of the mound, glittering with mica. All around it the wilderness ran riot, but not a leaf, stray vine or bird mess marred the shining surface.

I frowned as I stepped reluctantly closer. I could hear voices. The words were indecipherable; only the undulating rhythm could be discerned. The sound came from the mound, I realized – from the rocks. They were whispering.

"You must change your clothes," Mother said softly. "Open your pack."

I pressed my lips closed on the questions that wanted to escape, and instead took the pack from my shoulders. I pulled out a long white shift, belted with a twisted cord of gold. It was new, and must have been specially made for me; not many people needed a shift so long.

The night air shivered over my skin as I took off my cloak and gown and dropped the cool shift over my head. My mother took the cloak and reversed it so that the red lining was on the outside, glowing vividly in the half-light as she clasped it at my throat. She pressed a kiss to both my cheeks and I heard the quiet huff of her breath, slightly quicker than usual; then, with a last touch to my shoulder, Mama left me and walked forward to lay a hand on the lintel stone.

The rock whispering grew louder. More voices joined the first ones, their strange words mingling into a soft babble of sound. Around us, the forest seemed to fall still.

"You must pass through the gateway." Mama gestured to the waiting shadows within the opening.

"I..." My stomach fluttered. "Alone?"

"Yes," she answered. Her tone was even but her fingers curled into a fist on the stone.

I hesitated. Mama's face softened. "This must be done, my love," she said, so quietly that I could hardly hear the words. "But if I did not think you were ready, I would never send you through alone."

Send me through? Where was I going? I looked at Mama's face again. There was no trace of expression now. I knew she would not force me to do anything. She was waiting for me to make my decision.

I took a deep breath and stepped forward. Bending, I ducked my head and squeezed into the narrow opening under the horizontal slab. The dark enveloped me as if a hood had been thrown over my head; there was nothing except blackness. The sound of my breathing echoed as if in a much larger space, overlapping the whisper of the rocks. Then there was a hollow percussion, as if hands had clapped over my ears. My body seemed to jolt; my ears rang; and I blinked furiously as light shone suddenly into my face.

Eyes watering, I emerged from the darkness.

When I stood, it was not in a clearing in the forest but on a circular plateau at the crest of a hill. At regular intervals around the edge of the plateau were seven standing stones, each taller than a man; they thrust up into the belly of a turbulent sky that roiled with silver-purple storm clouds and irregular pulses of lightning. The stone chamber through which I had just crawled was at the centre of the circle.

The voices of seven women, echoing and overlapping, rose from the standing stones.

This is the Circle of Ancestors, and you are welcome here.

I gasped, stepped back involuntarily and bumped into the earth mound. Small workings I knew, and my mother's familiar gift; but the scale of the power in this place dwarfed and frightened me. It was all I could do to quaver out, "What – what must I do here?"

You must pass the test.

"Test? What test?"

There was no answer. The wind whistled across the hilltop, catching my hair and blowing the shift against my body. I drew the cloak more closely around me and waited for the stones to speak again.

They stayed silent.

Gradually, as nothing more frightening confronted

me, my tension eased. I began to look about with a little more interest. After a few more moments, I ventured from the safety of the earth mound to the edge of the plateau. The land spread below me like a tapestry, so clear I felt I could reach down and stroke the uneven bumpy smudges of forest and velvety patchwork of farmland. My eyes wandered to the jagged far-off peaks of the mountains and, still more distant, a thin grey rim on the horizon I was sure must be the sea.

The land at the foot of the hill was strange, distorted by a series of curved banks and ditches that made the earth seem to undulate gently beneath its green skin. Puzzled, I walked a little further along the plateau and looked down again. The same curved lines continued all the way around the base in a series of concentric circles, as if the hill had been dropped carelessly into the countryside and its landing had caused ripples in the earth. Such formations could not be natural, but why and how would men do such a thing?

I squinted at the ground, allowing my senses, which had narrowed defensively in my earlier fear, to sweep downwards. I felt for the enaid that should have been washing at random over the earth, and was stunned to discover that it was flowing through the spirals of land as tamely as a channelled river, funnelling into the base of the hill. I turned back to look at the plateau. Enaid welled up through the earth mound at the centre and wended in and out of the circle of stones.

"Who built all this?" I whispered.

The stones replied, *We did.*

I jumped again. After a moment's hesitation, I asked, "Who are you?"

We are the wise women who once ruled this land from the desert to the sea.

"Why did you create this place?"

So that a part of us might always live on here, and we might know our descendants.

I looked back down at the rippling earth in wonder. A gust of wind buffeted me and I reached out to steady myself on the nearest standing stone.

The instant my fingers made contact a sigh rose from the circle of stones. A shimmer like a heat haze rose with the sound, and suddenly I saw not smooth green ripples in the earth but the earth itself, laid open in its rich strata of black and brown. Hundreds of men and women scurried over the great earthworks, digging and carrying soil, working to complete the gargantuan pattern. Beneath my hand the cold stone warmed and softened, then flexed; I touched not rock but skin and cloth. I tried to snatch my fingers back, but they were caught and held in a firm grasp.

I looked up into calm green eyes set deep under auburn brows – my own eyes, but older, happier and serene. The woman gripped me with a wiry strength I recognized from my mother, her eyes gleaming with amusement.

"Hello. I am Angharad, your great-great-great-great-grandmother. Goodness, child! There's no need to look so worried. I know that where you have come from I am long dead, but that is all the more reason to rejoice in this opportunity to meet me. Here, such things are irrelevant."

I was looking at my own Ancestor. I didn't know if I should fall to my knees before her or simply beg her forgiveness for my intrusion. What was I doing here? This was no place for the youngest child of the king – the useless daughter. This was a place for real wise women and for Great workings. But no, no. I tried to collect myself, even as my scattered wits seemed to flutter about in the wind. Mother had sent me here. She must have had a reason.

"What must I do?" I managed.

"Do? You must listen, dear one. You are good at that ... perhaps too good. Look down again at the earth. You see the followers of the Old Ways, labouring to make this sacred place even more powerful. There are hundreds upon hundreds of them in this time. Look out over the forests and mountains, and at the sea."

Angharad turned me back to face the centre of the plateau. It was the same hilltop, but no standing stones had yet been placed here. The earth mound was still – or already – there. She drew me to it and sat down with a sigh of relief, bumping her heels idly against the sloping side. I perched beside her, noticing distantly that her hands and mine were the same; except that mine were perhaps a little smaller and less weathered. The blood of our line must run strongly indeed. The thought brought a sense of pride, even in my dazed state, and I sat up straight.

Angharad smiled as she observed this, and continued. "For a long time, wise women have been leaders of men. But just as the seasons must change, the nature of men cannot remain the same. Already the change has begun. Ambition has crept into the hearts of men. Soon, this land will no longer be united. Boundaries will be imposed, and people will come to believe that the land belongs to *them*. that it is their right to take as much as they can and call themselves its owner. You live in such times, do you not?"

My father's words, overheard long ago, echoed in my mind: *I rule this land. I am its master.*

"Yes. My father..." I stopped, not wanting to be disloyal.

"Oh, yes. I see it clearly," Angharad said, her gaze wistful. "I'm afraid it is inevitable. And your father, though lacking any sight beyond that of his eyes, is not a bad man. In his own way he loves his Kingdom." She stood, sweeping out her arms dramatically so that her cloak and gown swirled around her. "But we will make here a place where wise women will always be safe and welcome; a place where the enaid will always be strong, guarded by all the magical defenses at our disposal.

And when we have finished the earthworks we will bring here seven massive stones, taller than men. Each of the wise women will chose one stone and put something of herself into it – her strength, knowledge, the sorrows and joys that make her who she is – so that even after our mortal bodies have passed back into the earth, a part of us will remain."

I felt sadness sweep through me. Everything she had spoken of had come to pass. When I returned to my own time, all that would be left of her would be the stone on the hilltop.

I closed my eyes for a minute, reminding myself that there was a test to be passed. I took a deep breath and asked, "What is the test?"

Angharad smiled. "You have already passed it, dear one," she said. "Only a wise woman can awaken the Circle of Ancestors and pass back in time to speak with us."

I felt the blood drain from my face, leaving my cheeks cold. "What?" I gasped. "Me? But I'm not a real wise woman."

Her expression hardened. "You are your mother's daughter, Alexandra. It is in your name: 'helper of mankind'. You are a guardian of the land and a keeper of wisdom, and while that might seem a great burden, you cannot escape it. Your mother must have taught you this – you know what you are."

"She hasn't taught me anything of the sort!" I cried. "I'm only a cunning woman! I can't do Great workings, and I'd never even heard of the Circle of Ancestors until today. This is a mistake!"

Now it was Angharad's turn to be taken aback. "What?" she whispered. She reached out with one of her hardened hands and caught my fingers in hers. "But, my child ... something is very wrong here. Do you mean to tell me you know nothing of the heart of the land?"

I shook my head emphatically.

"And your mother told you nothing of what you have come here to experience? Nothing at all? You don't feel anything yourself? Have the slightest inkling?"

She was listening to me at last. Relieved, I shook my head once more.

"Oh dear." Angharad suddenly looked old and tired. "Oh dear. Your mother... Poor Branwen. She was the only one who ever failed..."

I blinked at her. What were we talking about now? She seemed to be lost in a kind of private reverie, muttering to herself. "I think I begin to see. Your father... I know he is not a kind man. And your mother wanted to protect you from more hurt – her own hurt... foolish, foolish, yes, but understandable ... and so she just sent you along. But you've never seen... Oh dear."

She turned back to me. "You have no idea who you are. What you are. But I can show you."

"I beg your pardon," I said with some dignity. "But I know who I am. I'm Lady Alexandra, youngest child of the king and Lady Branwen the Wise."

She smiled, amused. "I like that. But just wait..." She reached out her hands and placed them on either side of my head, thumbs resting above my eyebrows. "Just close your eyes."

I looked into her face and found myself obeying. My lids suddenly felt incredibly heavy and they closed almost involuntarily.

For a while, there was nothing but the quiet sound of our breathing and the whistle of the wind. Then something seemed to shift inside me. It felt as if my skin were humming; then I thought I was spilling out of myself, dissolving; and there was light, a pure white light...

The next moment I was falling back into myself, convulsing with pain. The world seemed to blur around me; Angharad and I both fell off the edge of the earth mound. I staggered up and cried out as pain stabbed my back and shoulder, running up my neck until I was half blind with it.

"No!" I only dimly heard Angharad's anguished voice.

Suddenly women's arms surrounded me – not just Angharad's but those of six more women. Dark and fair, tall and short, beautiful and plain, each woman seemed to cradle me. Seven sets of fingers stroked my face.

"We are sorry. So sorry." They whispered together. *"It's too late. We cannot help you anymore. We cannot keep you here. You are needed in your own place and time."*

There was an almighty jolt. I must have screamed but there was no sound. The light around me, the faces of the women who held me, winked out. I was engulfed in blackness, crushed by it, suffocating – then I found that I was merely lying on the dirt floor of the earth chamber and I struggled forward.

As soon as I emerged, dazed and gasping, into the shadowy clearing, I knew something was wrong. It was not what had happened in the Circle, nor the shadow of pain in my shoulder, that told me – I could smell it. Pain and fear hung in the air with a heavy stench like burnt flesh.

"Mama?" I whispered.

My voice seemed to evaporate in the darkness and my ears strained against the silence. I took shallow sips of air, hardly daring to move. I could not see her, but I could feel her presence, a ripple in the enaid, somewhere among the trees. I could feel something else too. Something rotted and black. Something that yearned and hated. Something that ... slithered. I gagged at the touch of it against my awareness.

Then there was a sharp, high scream, cut off abruptly.

"Mama!" I yelled, throwing myself into the forest.

I crashed into the blackness of the dense trees, and headed blindly for my mother's voice, forging a path through the whipping leaves and low boughs.

I stumbled over her. She was crumpled on the forest floor, face down. Her shoulder glistened with dark liquid in the dim light. I by her side, my arms going round her to lift her against my chest. She groaned softly, her eyelids flickering.

"No ... heart..." she whispered. "Go ... must ... please..." She was barely conscious. I could feel the warmth of her blood trickling through my fingers and pooling around my knee. There was a rush of movement in the forest behind me. I snapped around, twisting as far as I could without releasing Mama, and caught a glimpse of something low to the ground and gleaming dark red as it flashed through a gap in the trees. An instant later, I caught another flash of chestnut and a terrifying blur of teeth in the undergrowth to my right.

The thing was circling us.

Mama groaned with pain, and terror raked down my spine like claws. The dreadful warm wetness was seeping through my shift. There was another glint of chestnut, this time to my left and much closer.

In my panic and fear I did something – I'm still not sure how – somehow reached down into the earth and pushed it away, flung Mama and myself forward. The claustrophobic darkness of the forest, the looming shadows and the creature that moved among them disappeared; a screaming, flailing wind seemed to tear them away, and thrust another landscape into their place.

Dizzily I looked up. It was near dawn; the sky was blushing a delicate silver behind the Hall. The beautiful, familiar shapes of my mother's plants and trees were all around us. We were home.

I started screaming.

CHAPTER
THREE

It was a few minutes before the first members of the household found us. Those minutes were the most excruciating I have ever lived through. At first it seemed that my screams went unheard. Nothing moved; there was no reply – and fear that somehow I was alone made me scream all the louder. Then came the first stirrings, the first sleepy voices, and the first flickers of light as tapers were lit. There were running footsteps, doors banging open, and at long last someone came.

It was Robin. When he saw us he went white as bone and almost fell down beside me, his shaking fingers hovering over Mother's face as he added his voice to mine, shouting for help.

After that everything became a blur. The rest of the household arrived, crying out and asking questions, prising my mother's limp body from my hold, and carrying her into the Hall. I stayed with them, refusing to let go of Mama's hand when we reached her bedchamber and she was gently laid down on the bed.

My father appeared beside us and dragged me away, his fingers gripping my shoulder hard enough to bruise. "What happened, girl?" he demanded. "What in the name of the Ancestors happened?"

"I ... I don't know." I couldn't tell him the truth; I couldn't tell him of the sacred Circle of Ancestors. "We – we went for a walk. In the forest. Something attacked us."

"What attacked you? Who?"

"A thing – an animal. I never saw. It was too fast," I stammered.

He shook his head in disgust and released my shoulder to bend over Mother's prone form, his jaw clenched. The women of the household fluttered and fussed around us.

For a few minutes I simply stood there, exhaustion and the daze of shock fogging my mind. Then the inane, frightened chatter of the women penetrated my consciousness. They plucked at her bloodstained clothes, tapped her face with shaking hands, while my father looked on helplessly.

My mother was the one who cared for the sick, who was strong when there was a crisis. There were two cunning women here, but they were used to Mother directing their small gifts. Without her they were all lost, even my father.

I snapped back into focus, my mind sharpening into a spear point of determination. I waded through the crowd to the bedside.

"Quiet!" I shouted. My voice was shrill with urgency and they obeyed instantly. I gathered my thoughts, then spoke again, pointing at a serving woman. "You – fetch me water, but make sure it is well boiled first. Rosabel and Elswyth, go to my mother's workroom and bring me her book – the large brown one – her pestle and mortar, the glass jar with the picture of a spider on it, and all the bandages you can find. Melle, take a basket and go into the gardens, you will see a tall leafy plant with small yellow flowers. Pick both the flowers and the leaves, at least three handfuls. You will see also a circle of small fragrant plants with silver leaves: pull one up and bring me the roots. And bring a handful of berries from the dark green bush that grows along the south wall. Be quick!"

The women, still shocked but grateful for something to do, fled. The two cunning women remained, along with four men and my father.

"You two" – I pointed at the women – "you can help me here. The rest of you must leave; we need space and quiet to work."

My father opened his mouth as if to protest. I glared at him, daring him – almost willing him – to try to gainsay me. He shut his lips, his jaw clenching; then his gaze dropped and he turned and strode from the room, the other men at his back.

With the help of the two cunning women I turned Mama over, and cut away her ruined gown. The women made worried noises at the amount of blood around the wound. I used the ripped remains of the gown to apply pressure to it, but I was less worried about loss of blood than the awful carrion stench coming from the injury. It was the smell that had hung in the air in the forest.

A moment later the other women, flushed with running, arrived back with the ingredients I had asked for and Mama's book. It was time to clean the wound. I peeled off the wad of cloth and braced myself for what was to come.

The gash was a ragged semicircle in the top of Mother's shoulder. It was not very wide – not even the span of one of my hands – but it was extremely deep. So deep that I knew nerves and muscles must have been severed. Mother might never use this arm again. My hands, busily grinding crowberries, fell still as horror seized me. Ancestors – she could be crippled for the rest of her life. I had no idea how to prevent it. I couldn't do this! I gritted my teeth and forced the panic from my mind. I *had* to do this. There was no choice.

The first time I cleaned out the bloody, gaping wound, something burst inside it – a sac of foul yellow-green poison that ate through the bandage like acid and filled the air with a smell of rotting flesh so intense that I gagged. The women helping me leaped back with dismayed cries. I dropped the bandage but stayed where I was, grimly pouring more water into the gash and probing deep into the wound until all the poison had gone. Then I got up, washed my hands, went back and cleaned it out again.

I nursed my mother day and night. I used every healing potion I knew and a few I invented, applied poultice after poultice, and poured draughts and tisanes down her throat on the hour. I used every healing charm I could remember or imagine. I reached into the tides that flowed through the Hall and drew as much from them as my skin could hold, then poured it out into Mama's body. But I had a worrying feeling that the power was simply seeping out of her; I had no Great gift to anchor it there.

I refused to leave her side, even for a moment. My father and brothers came and went, each taking a turn to be with Mother and I. Robin coaxed me into eating and tried to make me rest. Hugh came and told jokes, inappropriate and feeble, to try to make me smile, though his own lips never curved and his gaze never left Mother's face. David had nothing to say, but he was always there to help me hold Mother when she thrashed and struggled on the bed. My father did nothing but stand at the foot of the bed and watch us, his eyes despairing and his fists clenched.

I knew they were suffering too, that they loved her and feared for her as I did. I knew they also worried about me. But I saw them only peripherally. I had to concentrate on Mama. Tending to her drove me to the very end of my strength and I had nothing to spare for them.

Something had happened in the forest that I did not understand. Mama had been attacked by ... something ... and she had lost a lot of blood, yes. The wound had also been poisoned or infected. But still – I had stopped the bleeding, and cleared out the poison. A wound of this kind was dangerous but surely not life-threatening – especially not to someone of Mother's vibrant health. Everything I knew, everything the book told me, said that Mama should be mending.

She did not mend.

That first day she stirred a great deal, opening her eyes to speak to me. She was confused, seeming to think that we were still in the forest, urging me to run and trying to get up. The second day she became less lucid, rambling and fighting us, calling out my name and those of my father and brothers. On the third day she quietened, and though she mumbled and cried out she did not wake. Her always pale skin had become translucent, the veins standing out like snaking bruises.

On the fourth day I woke from a restive doze and lifted my head from the pillow of my arms where I sat slumped over the bed. It was barely dawn and I was the only one in the room. My mother was quiet. The sun had swept golden fingers over her face, giving it a rosy glow. I gazed at her, feeling a flicker of hope in my heart. She looked peaceful.

Tiredly, I reached for the echo of her life to reassure myself. I couldn't feel it.

She was not breathing.

That night, as the sun sank behind the hills, we burned my mother.

Robin stood behind me, his hands on my shoulders. David and Hugh flanked me, each holding one of my hands. They crowded close, not just for comfort, but to keep me from falling. Father stood on the other side of the pyre, his eyes on the flames. He was nothing more than a pale-faced smudge in the deepening night.

The world was a muddle of black shapes limned in fiery orange. As the sparks spiralled upwards, I wanted more than anything to follow them away into the cool numbness of the sky. I felt hollow inside, scraped out and aching, and my eyes were gritty and dry. I had no more tears left.

My mother was dead.

Part of me refused to believe it, even as I watched the fire crackle and leap. And yet somehow it was as if it had always been true, as if all my years had been lived in that one day, and I had been born already crying with grief.

As the sun slipped away, the fire died down. When it was dark, my brothers led me back to the Hall. Robin came into my room with me and, as if I were a baby again, he found my nightgown for me, and brushed and braided my tangled hair. When I climbed into bed, he tucked the blankets around me. For a few moments he sat on the edge of the sunken bed, looking away from me. The quiet seemed to swell around us, heavy with unshed tears.

At last he rose and lit a candle to leave burning beside me, though that darkness had never held fears for me before. He pressed a kiss to my forehead, whispered, "Sleep well, dear one," and went, closing the door behind him.

Then I found that there were tears left in me still.

CHAPTER
FOUR

The days that followed the burning were bleak. The servants and people of the household wandered about like ghosts. We were lost.

David was twenty by then, and Hugh eighteen, but they joined Robin in looking after me, spending all their time in my company without a word of complaint and seeing to my needs with the dedication of nursemaids. In truth, I believe that their concern for me gave them something other than grief to dwell on, and an excuse to cluster together; for we craved one another's warmth in the coldness that seemed to have sunk over the Hall.

I never ventured into Mother's gardens. I could not bear the sight of them. The plants were dying, withering away into crumbled mould, succumbing to insects, parasites and fungi. They couldn't live without her.

Neither could we. We barely saw Father. He seemed to have forgotten he had children. Gone was the dedicated ruler I knew, the hearty and sometimes affectionate father my brothers loved. Perhaps it was only after Mama had gone that he realized how much he had loved her; or perhaps regret for all the harsh words between them haunted him. I do not know. The morning after we burned Mama, Father took his bow and his spears and went out into the forest alone. He returned long after dark, weary and sore, his arms covered in thin scratches as if he had been crawling through the undergrowth. He went out the next day, and the next. No one offered to go with him, nor did anyone question why he returned exhausted night after night without so much as a rabbit to show for it.

We all knew why he went.

He spoke to me only once in that first week, to ask me more details about the creature I had seen so fleetingly. His eyes stayed fixed on the mantel behind me the entire time, and when I was finished he walked away without another word. His face was like granite and I dared not try to stop him; but I shivered with dread at the thought of my father coming face to face with the beast. I knew far better than he how strong it must have been to best Mother, and that such strength could not be natural. No creature formed from the earth had such noxious venom or such terrifying speed. He could not hope to defeat it.

But that first week turned into another, and another, and Father still returned each night after dark empty-handed – and unhurt. I let myself hope that the creature, whatever it had been, had disappeared as silently and malevolently as it had come. Eventually I began to feel safe again.

Then came a day when Father returned long before dark – and he was not empty-handed.

Robin and I were sat in the long room, I on the rug by his feet with my head against his knee. He stroked my hair idly, but neither of us spoke, instead listening to David as he consulted the steward. In Father's absence David had been forced to take on many of his daily duties to keep everything in order. Hugh had gone out a few minutes earlier, and I could sense his presence somewhere near the stables. Whenever he was not with us, he was usually with his falcons and horses, as if he couldn't bear to be in the Hall alone.

Suddenly there was a commotion outside. We heard running footsteps in the courtyard and our father's raised voice. As Robin and I stiffened and David rose from his chair, Hugh burst through the doors.

"It's Father," he said, out of breath. "And there's a woman; I think she's hurt. Quickly, Alexa."

I scrambled up and followed him, the other two on my heels as I ran out into the sunlight, blinking. I saw my father at the centre of a crowd of people, mostly men of the household, and stopped dead in the doorway.

Father's face was more animated than I had ever seen it, filled with an excitement that lit his eyes and smoothed away the lines of age and care. He looked like a man who had seen the sun for the first time in years. The expression so changed him that I felt a whisper of alarm brush along my spine, and it was only when David bumped into me that I moved forward. The crowd parted before me and I saw for the first time the woman my father cradled in his arms.

She was sleeping, or unconscious, and slumped against Father's chest like a child, tiny in comparison with his bulk. The filmy fabric of her dress stretched taut over full curves at breast and hip, and her face was a lovely oval with plump lips and long dark lashes. Her skin was golden and her hair cascaded down her back in a shining fall of perfectly straight honey brown. As I stood there, a breeze ruffled the fine strands of hair and sent them blowing over Father's shoulder into a ray of sunlight. As the light caught in it, I saw the deep chestnut glint in the depths of her glorious locks.

My breath stopped. I knew where I had seen that colour before.

Father noticed me. "Good. Run into the Hall, child, and have a room made ready. And fetch your healing plants and such." His tone was urgent but I was rooted to the spot, still staring at the flare of bloody colour in her hair.

"Go on, girl!" he roared.

I shook myself and went mechanically back into the Hall to find servants and give them Father's instructions. Then I ventured into my mother's workroom and reluctantly chose healing and reviving draughts from among the mixtures on the shelves. But even as my eyes pricked with tears at the familiar sight and smells of the room, my mind was running back over the scene in the courtyard – remembering the look in my father's eyes and the chestnut in the woman's hair.

Moments later, Father carried the woman into the newly prepared chamber and laid her down on the bed with a gentleness I had thought entirely foreign to his nature. My brothers followed him in, their faces showing a confusion that echoed mine.

"Look after her," Father ordered me. "Make her well. Give her whatever she needs."

"But who is she, Father?" asked Hugh. He shifted uneasily; I could tell he was as disturbed as I was by the possessive note in Father's normally controlled voice.

"Yes, and where did you find her?" David said seriously, his fingers tapping restively on the bedpost. I went to the table beside the bed and, with Robin's help, unpacked my basket of herbs as I listened to Father's reply.

Father began with a great booming laugh that sounded almost giddy. "I was hunting, and I caught sight of something; I thought it was the creature that Alexandra said she had seen. I threw a spear and missed; but instead of running, the thing circled, and I followed. It led me a pretty dance, and I chased it for two hours, all to no avail. It finally disappeared, too clever for me in the end. I suppose that's the last we'll see of it." He laughed again, carelessly. "I found myself in a part of the forest I had never seen before, and there I wandered, thoroughly lost. Then I heard a sound. A voice. It was so beautiful that it seemed to stop my heart. It called my name, sang to me inside my head, led me to the edge of a clearing. And there she lay, sleeping. Waiting for me."

"You mean ... you haven't even spoken to her?" David said, aghast.

Father laughed exuberantly, clasping David's shoulder. "Son, don't you see? There's no need. She's mine. Made for me."

I looked down at the woman. Her head was turned away from me and she was perfectly still – her eyelids did not flicker, nor did her deep, even breaths falter – but suddenly I was sure that she was awake, listening to everything that was being said. I glanced at Robin and saw suspicion on his face.

"I do not think this sleep is natural," I said aloud. "Perhaps I should try black root."

Anyone with the faintest knowledge of herbs knows black root has such a foul stench that it will usually induce vomiting. I met Robin's eyes and waited.

The woman's breathing hitched; then she began to stir. Her soft hands slid along the sheet, the long delicate fingers fluttering. I noted with dislike that neither a freckle nor a callus marred them.

My father was beside her in an instant, clasping one of those beautiful hands. "Do you wake, my love?" he asked. "There is nothing to fear; I am with you." His cooing tone filled me with revulsion.

The woman opened her eyes.

Robin's head jerked, but he stood fast at my side. Both Hugh and David involuntarily backed away, David making a muffled sound of shock. I gasped, almost choking as the woman's presence expanded into the room like the rich, sickly stench of carrion released from a bloated, rotting body. Her power flooded my senses until it seemed to drum against the walls, deafening, maddening.

Somehow the foul power had the opposite effect on Father. Spellbound, he leaned closer still. She gazed wordlessly up into his face, and slowly he reached out one of his great clumsy hands and brushed a strand of hair from her cheek. She smiled. Father sucked in an awed breath at the sight.

Then her eyes turned on me. No speck of light reflected from their surface; they were as flat and black as shadows. Her gaze met mine with a force like a hammer blow. I nearly staggered as her will bore down on me. I had never before met such strength, such a relentless, ravenous will – such hunger to crush and destroy. It terrified me.

No. Defiance surged, giving me the strength to stare back. I would *not* bend. I would *not* look away.

Slowly, painfully, I took a step closer to the bed, pushing back with all my might; but her will seemed implacable. I gritted my teeth, pushed harder. I felt something give.

An expression of boredom crossed her face, and her gaze flicked away.

I swayed at the sudden release of pressure. Robin steadied me, and I sagged gratefully against his arm. My eyelids felt stiff; I blinked furiously. Who was this woman? *What* was she?

She returned her attention to my father, smiling up into his besotted face.

"What is your name?" he asked.

"I am Zella." Her voice was deep for a woman's, melodious and rich.

"Shadow..." I muttered limply.

"What?" Robin whispered in my ear.

"Zella is an old word for shadow."

"How did you come to be in the forest, Zella?" Father asked gently.

She sighed, looking up at him through her luxuriant lashes. "I know not. I have slumbered for long and long. But even as I slept, my heart searched for the one I was awaiting ... the one who could awaken me. I remember nothing more."

I turned to meet the incredulous looks of David and

 57

Hugh. Robin shook his head. Would Father really believe this sickening rubbish?

"Zella..." he murmured. "I feel I have slumbered also, waiting for you."

The long room filled with people half an hour before my father had summoned them to arrive. News travelled fast in the Hall – and all the household people wanted a look at this woman who, it was rumoured, had bewitched him. My brothers and I had taken the chairs by the mantel, and avoided the anxious stares of the people arriving. We had no reassurance to give.

Father had sent us from the room within minutes of Zella's awakening, and remained closeted with her there for the best part of the afternoon. As early evening fell he had called a handful of the household men in, and there had been a flurry of activity, with this gathering called.

As we waited for him to arrive, servants and cooks began to filter in from the kitchens, laying out the long tables and bringing with them a stunning assortment of food. There were delicacies which I had only seen once or twice in my life: spiced rice from the far south of the continent, saffron-coloured sweets, a roasted peacock (the sight of which made me turn away with a shudder). Still Father and the woman did not arrive. The noise in the long room gradually changed from worried whispering to resentful mutters. There was fear in the low-pitched voices, in the emphatic, broken-off gestures and in the sharp looks of the gathered people. Through it all, my brothers and I could only wait, keeping our unhappy concern to ourselves. We knew that something was very wrong, but not what it was, or what could be done about it.

There was a ripple of sound – surprise? wonder? – from outside the hall where those not invited to the gathering had crammed themselves, waiting. The babble of sighs and excited voices spread, swelling into the long room and stirring the crowd to a swirl of movement. I stood, hearing my brothers follow suit behind me, but the shifting mass in front of us kept the hub of the excitement from our sight.

Then the rank of people before us parted – and we saw what they had seen.

It was Zella. She stood arm in arm with Father, attired in a flowing gown of garnet-coloured velvet. With a jolt of stunned revulsion, I recognized it as one of Mother's, hastily altered. Mother's rubies glittered at her ears; Mother's coral comb fastened the honey-coloured hair in an elegant sweep. She looked unspeakably lovely, young and glowing in the evening light. For the merest instant her gaze brushed mine – and her lips curved in a smile that was not young at all. She lifted one of her hands, glittering with my mother's rings, and stroked her fingers lovingly along the deep neckline of the gown. Then her face was turned back up to my father's, a delicate flush staining her round cheeks.

I did not realize I had stepped forward until Robin's hands closed over my shoulders and held me still.

"Don't be stupid," he hissed.

Before I could argue, David and Hugh were flanking me, their grave faces bidding me to silence. I stopped straining against Robin's hands, and saw something that doused my anger like sand poured over a candle.

Wherever Zella looked, a change was occurring. The set, resentful faces of the household people were transformed, softening into expressions of smiling happiness. I saw every eye go blank, every furrowed brow unwrinkle. There was a burst of spontaneous laughter that spread and turned suddenly into applause.

At that moment I believe I was more frightened than I had ever been in my life – more frightened even than the night Mama had been attacked. For we were under attack again now, and this time there was nowhere to run. I did not know what Zella was doing, or how it was possible, but she was taking them. Our people. She was taking them all.

Father strode past us without a backward glance, drawing Zella to the head table, where the roasted peacock's tail feathers had been set in my mother's favourite vase.

"My people!" he roared. "My loyal people. I have called you here to share in my joy. The Ancestors have sent me an unparalleled gift – one I only hope I may prove to be worthy of, in time. Let me present to you all the Lady

Zella." He paused dramatically. "She has consented to be my wife!"

There was a roar of approval and more applause from the gathered people. I leaned against Robin, my knees shaking too much to hold me upright. His arm around me was like a band of iron.

"Ancestors..." I heard Hugh's shaken whisper, and saw, as I turned my head, the tears filming his eyes. David stood like a pillar of rock, his face so hard that he looked more like Father than I had ever seen him.

In the midst of the noise and confusion, I saw Zella stand on tiptoe and whisper something in Father's ear. He looked surprised for a moment, then, for the first time since he had entered the long room, he turned to his children, huddled against the mantel. He spread his arms wide, and quiet fell again as the crowd waited for him to speak. "Come, children," he called to us. "You must embrace your new mother."

There was unreal silence. At my sides, my hands clenched slowly into fists, and this time Robin laid no restraining fingers on my shoulder. But it was David – calm, sensible David – who spoke, his cheeks darkening with rage. "Our mother is dead."

Before Father could react, Zella stepped forward, smiling. "Yes," she agreed calmly. "But now I am here."

CHAPTER
FIVE

That night my brothers and I sat on my bed, the shadows flickering about us. The darkness was filled with fear and doubt, strange voices whispering that we tried not to hear.

In less than a day Zella had conquered the household. She had won over all our people; anyone who was in her presence for more than a few minutes left her company wide-eyed and convinced of her perfection. The few visitors who had been present from other villages and farms had galloped off to spread the news of her arrival with unfocused expressions of bliss. She held Father in the palm of her hand.

How long would it be before she held the whole Kingdom?

"What I don't understand is why she hasn't tried to

enchant *us*," said Hugh. "She's taken control of everyone else, but we still see her for what she is."

Robin answered for me. "She tried. Didn't she, Alexa? I felt it when she first woke – you must have too, Hugh. It was like … being drowned. What *I* don't understand is why it didn't work."

I rested my chin on my drawn-up knees. "I think it's Mother. Her blood in us. It makes us different, gives us the strength to resist Zella – if not defeat her." I paused, then whispered, "If Mother were here that woman could never have entered this house."

There was a long silence as my brothers absorbed those words. The same thought was in each of our heads, buzzing in the air between us. Finally, I said it. "I think … I think Zella was the thing that killed Mama."

Abruptly David stood. "We need to find Father. Get him away from her, alone. If we talk to him, surely we can make him see sense."

I shook my head. "No, it's no use, David. He's besotted. Her grip on him is the strongest of all."

Robin snorted. "No wonder," he said bitterly. "She obviously knows his nature well."

"What?" David looked at us searchingly. "What do you mean?"

Robin shrugged and Hugh didn't meet my gaze, so I explained wearily. "Think, David. Mother and Father fought like stags in the mating season almost all my life. Mama was tall and strong, with a temper and a fierce will. He couldn't bend her and it drove him mad. But Zella, now ... she's tiny and outwardly sweet, and she agrees with everything he says. Mama had pale skin and fiery hair; Zella has golden skin and hair like honey. Mama had calloused, ugly hands; Zella has fine, soft ones." I looked down at my own stubby freckled fingers. "He'd be in love with her even if she had never cast a spell."

David's mouth pressed into a thin line and he sat back down on the bed. "Damn him. Damn him for an old fool."

"Think, Alexa," Robin urged. "This is all magic, and if there's one thing you know it's magic. You're as strong as her – you stood against her and won."

"No, I didn't," I said grimly. "And no, I'm not. She's far stronger than I could ever be. What she's done here is a Great working. But..."

Hugh leaned forward. "Go on."

"I don't think – no, I'm *sure* that the form she holds now is not her natural one. I don't think she's human." They stared at me, and I rushed on. "I think her *real* shape is that of the beast which killed Mama. If that's true, she could not possibly hold her disguise as a woman without aid, not for such a long period as she was closeted with Father this afternoon. An enchantment that complex would drain her completely. Even Mama couldn't have done such a working without help."

I stopped and thought. "She must have a talisman. A magical object to keep her shape-changing spells confined within."

"A talisman?"

"What object?"

"I don't know." I rubbed my forehead tiredly. "It could be anything. But since she came here with only the clothes on her back, it must be something small, something she can hold or conceal. Perhaps a ring? And she will keep it close to her at all times. If it were destroyed she would be forced to revert to her true form."

David nodded decisively. "And even Father couldn't be blind to that. Somehow we must find this talisman." He paused, and then said thoughtfully, "Father intends to marry her in three days, but until they are wed she sleeps alone. Could we steal into her bedchamber while she sleeps and search for it?"

"What if she were to wake?" Hugh asked.

"It's too dangerous," said Robin, shaking his head. "Perhaps we could trick it from her?"

"No trick would make her give it up. She will always be aware of it, guarding it – except when she sleeps." I sat up straight. "I think I know a way to lessen the danger. Mama sometimes made up strong vapours that would send the gravely injured into a deep sleep so that the body could heal. If I made an infusion and it was placed in her room just after she fell asleep, the vapours would steal into her nose and throat and make her slumber so deeply that she would not wake even if you shook her. To search the room we would have to cover our own faces with cloths dipped in water – and be quick, for the vapours would, even so, affect us in less than half an hour."

"How will we recognize the talisman?" asked Hugh.

"I'll feel it. Don't worry about that."

The earliest the required potion could be prepared was the next night and we decided that we should put our plans into action as soon as it was ready.

Perhaps we should have waited, planned more thoroughly; but unspoken between us was the knowledge that time was slipping away faster than we could see. If we did not act soon, it would be too late.

Night had fallen. The powerful mixture of herbs and dried plants was ready, as were the cloths to cover our faces. Zella, with a very pretty curtsy, had pleaded tiredness and left the long hall for her bedchamber nearly an hour ago. All that day my brothers and I had watched her dominion over the household tighten. It seemed that Father fell more and more deeply under her spell every instant.

Preparations for their marriage were well in hand. The women of the household chattered and giggled, almost insensible with excitement at the prospect. The grey and black of mourning that they had all been wearing was packed away and forgotten, replaced by the brightness of summer gowns. New maids and servants were already being summoned from the outlying villages to help with the massive event, for Father wanted to claim his new bride before the whole of the Kingdom.

Through it all Zella smiled sweetly, her dark eyes flat and unblinking, even as she managed a charming blush at my father's touch on her arm.

Our resolve could be no stronger. It was time.

I gave Robin the ceramic vapour dish with its mesh lid and instructed him how to light it so that the distilled herbs would burn and the vapours would spill out. He was the most sure-footed of us, and would have the task of placing the dish in the chamber.

The muffled sound of our steps seemed unbearably loud as we made our way down the corridor. The passage was deserted, and a disconsolate silence lay over the Hall, though it was barely midnight. No one bothered staying awake after Zella had retired. What would be the point?

We reached the end of the passage in which Zella's chamber lay without seeing another soul. This was as we had hoped; yet the sensation of moving through an abandoned place made me shiver.

I reached up to tie one of the dampened cloths over Robin's face, fussing with the knot until he brushed my hands away. "Leave it," he whispered.

We clustered round the door, listening for any sound within. I did not dare reach into her room through the enaid in case she felt my encroachment and woke. We still had so little idea of the extent of her powers. I could feel her there, the high-pitched buzz of her presence like the whine of a maddened wasp; but the noise seemed subdued – not active.

"Very well," I whispered finally. "Open the door."

We stood back as Robin crouched below the handle, reaching up with his free hand to ease it down. He held the door as it opened slightly, pressing his eye to the gap. We waited for another moment, then he looked at us and nodded. He slid through the gap and into the darkness beyond.

I pressed myself against the wall next to the door, as if by willpower I might be able to see through it, and held my breath; but, only a few seconds later, he emerged and gently shut the door behind him.

"She was asleep. I did as you said, Alexa."

"Then we wait," I said.

We huddled round the entrance, stiff with tension and praying that no one would come this way and disturb us. The irony of our stealing about like thieves in our own home did not escape us, but we did not know if the household people would defend Zella against us. Had her power gone that deep? The thought of our own people turning on us was so alien that it made me feel sick, but the possibility could not be discounted. Both David and Robin had stout cudgels pushed into their belts, and Hugh his dagger. If we were successful tonight, they would never have to use them.

Eventually I judged that enough time had passed and nodded. We tied the cloths around our faces and opened the door. David went first, nodding that it was all right to follow before he disappeared inside. Robin kept me firmly behind him as he followed Hugh. Once we were all in, David closed the door.

The room was filled with a looming darkness that the dim starlight, falling from the windows opposite, did little to dispel. For a moment we remained together by the door, staring at our tormentor.

Unsurprisingly, Zella had been given the finest room in the Hall. Many years ago, when the ruler of the principality bordering us – Midland – had visited, he had been given this chamber and had expressed his pleasure with it. The greatest glory was the bed. Placed in the centre of the room, it was made of ancient black oak, sunk beautifully into the floor, its four thick posts hung with red and gold draperies. The plentiful cloth hid Zella completely from view.

The scent of the infusion that burned beside the bed, heady even through the cloth tied over my nose and mouth, recalled me to our task. I glanced at my brothers and gestured for them to separate and search. We could not risk lingering. As they scattered to look in the chests and closets, I approached the bed. I had not told my brothers the one fear I had which might ruin our plan: that Zella might sleep with the talisman, whatever it was, clutched tight in her hand. If that were the case then one of us would need to brave the bed to get it, if indeed it could be got.

I hesitated beside the drapes, shuddering as I heard the low hiss of breath issuing from beneath them. It sounded unnervingly like the noise of a snake. The high, irritating buzz of her power made it more difficult than I had thought to locate any separate aura, such as the one a talisman might emit.

I had to get closer.

Carefully I ducked under the nearest swathe of gold fabric and kneeled next to the bed. Zella lay at the exact centre of the mattress, surrounded by a tangled nest of cushions, furs and blankets. She was curled into a tiny ball with her knees drawn up to her chest and her face turned away from me. Her position reminded me of a wild creature. The vibration of power around her seemed dormant; but somehow in sleep it was stronger, as if in private she felt no need to restrain it. I could see the sheen of her hair as it spilled over the heaped pillows, and the smooth texture of the skin on the nape of her neck. The hiss of her breath was louder beneath the roof of cloth. Every fine hair on my body was standing up, my muscles quivering, my breathing coming in quick, shallow puffs.

Then my attention was caught by something. Zella's tiny, delicate feet were not hidden under the masses of bedding that covered the rest of her; they poked out from beneath a dark fur, with only a swirl of filmy bronze fabric tucked around them. I recognized that fabric. It was the same dress she had worn when Father carried her into the Hall the first time.

My brow wrinkled. Why, with all the fine laces and muslins that must have been offered to her, would she choose to sleep in that? Taking my courage firmly in hand, I reached out and caught one edge of the fabric and gently, gently, tugged it out from around her feet, keeping my eyes all the while on her back. She did not stir. Encouraged, I lifted up the dark fur and carefully pushed it aside, then took hold of a little more of the bronze material and pulled it free. Slowly I managed to free the whole hem of the garment and, forcing my hands to steadiness so that they would not so much as brush her skin, ran my fingers along it. Where the seam ran down the dress and met the one around the bottom, I found it.

It was a lump, slightly too big and too heavy to be mere clumsy stitching. When I touched it I felt a low hum of power, contained and even, like a carefully woven working should be. I wormed one of my fingers into the stitching and ripped it open in a single movement.

A tiny pebble dropped into my hand, nothing more than a river stone, worn smooth by rushing water. It was oval, dark grey, with a jagged line of white quartz crossing its centre. It pulsed in my palm like a miniature heart, making my fingers twitch and shake as they closed over it. Then there was a blast of bloody red light from the pebble. It jumped from my hand like a living thing and landed on Zella's neck, scurrying across her cheek to her face.

I was up and a foot away from the bed before I even realized I'd moved, opening my mouth to shout. But it was already too late. The buzz of Zella's power shifted into a high-pitched shriek of rage.

Red light exploded through the room. There was a concussion that shook the walls, made the ground itself heave, and I screamed in agony. Ancestors, the pain... The bones in my head seemed to splinter and the fragments pierce my brain. I collapsed, paralysed, as my mind flooded with horrific images – like a nightmare, except that I knew what I saw was real, was truly happening, as I lay helpless to prevent it.

I saw my brothers' faces twist and melt, saw them warped and misshapen, their skin bubbling, their bodies mutilated and broken, heard them screaming and the crack of their bones as Zella tortured them. I tried to reach into the enaid, tried to find some power to protect them, but I could not find the tide; the red power held it away. I reached out desperately and closed the fingers of my mind over my brothers' dying bodies.

There was a burst of pale light and they were gone, hidden from me. As their voices faded to silence I saw great white things – like clouds – soaring away into the sky. Birds, I realized as their massive wings pounded the air. Swans...

In the few seconds before darkness claimed me, the wing beats seemed to echo the rhythm of my heart.

CHAPTER
SIX

I drifted in a numbing darkness, weary beyond belief. In the darkness I heard voices murmuring, felt the touch of rain, smelled the sweet, intoxicating scent of roses and tasted salt; but I understood none of it.

Occasionally I would see light, and move painstakingly towards it. If I reached it before it disappeared, I would find myself back in my body, aching and weighed down by my own limbs. Perhaps I stirred or moaned, for whenever I forced open my eyes, indistinct faces would hover over me. But they were not my brothers. And then would come the sharp, bitter smell of herbs as something burning was poured into my mouth. I would choke as it slid down, then find myself back in the darkness.

It was the cool, sweet breeze blowing across my face that finally woke me. I was being rocked gently as I lay, and my breath ruffled the fluffy wool beneath my cheek so that it tickled my lips.

For a few minutes these physical sensations were enough; I was happy to curl into the warmth of the blankets wrapped around me and savour the good smell of the air. But eventually sounds began to penetrate my lethargy. The jingle of bit and harness, the thud and bump of wheels rumbling over the ground and the ricket and squeak of a wooden trap; and, with them, the slow seep of memory.

I lay still, my not quite alert mind turning over all that had occurred, trying to fit it together, until the importance of one question became paramount.

Where was I?

With weary, creaking movements that cost a frightening amount of energy, I wriggled over onto my back. I thought I saw something in the sky, a flock of great birds – swans or geese – their wings shadowed against the clouds; but before I could focus on them, they were gone. I reached up a leaden hand to grip the wooden rail and tried to pull myself up, my strength failed me halfway and I collapsed back onto the seat.

The sound of my efforts attracted the attention of the person driving the little wagon; the rocking motion slowed to a gentle halt, and a blissfully familiar face appeared. It was John, one of the household people, whom I had known all my life.

"Ah – 'ee's awake at last. Hold there, Lady, I'll be with

you in no time." He tied up the reins and clambered into the back of the trap.

"Where..." My voice was hoarse and gruff, and I had to stop and swallow before I could begin again. "Where am I?"

"Best have a drink and something to eat first, Lady. You'll feel better for it." He rummaged under the seat, pulling out a large basket from which he took cold cheese-stuffed potatoes, apple pasties, bread and a flask of small beer.

As the smell of food reached me my stomach let out a prolonged rumble and I realized I was famished. John saw my hungry look and passed me an apple pasty before slicing up the potatoes and bread.

"There now, it's a right lovely thing to see you eating again. You've even got roses in your cheeks."

I was too busy devouring the food to reply. I gulped the beer so quickly that I choked. Why was I so hungry and thirsty?

As soon as the last mouthful was swallowed, I drew the blankets close around me and fixed John with a severe look. "Now, where am I? What has happened?"

"Well, we're in Southfield. And you've been ill – 'tis no wonder you're as weak as a kitten."

"Ill?" I searched my memory. I remembered entering Zella's room and finding the talisman. There had been a warning spell on it, and it had got away from me. Then everything became blurry. I could remember the flash of red light, and dreadful pain ... and something white, something like clouds – but nothing else. Nothing that made sense. It was all like a nightmare. "For how long?"

"Nearly three days. You could barely open your eyes."

Three days since that night? I took a deep breath. "What happened to my brothers?"

John's pleasant face hardened into grim lines. "Them three." He spat. "Don't you be worrying about them. They won't be troubling the Kingdom again."

I was stunned. My brothers had always been friends to this man, helping him in the barn from toddling age. He'd put them on their first mounts. That he should speak their names with such dislike...

"John, tell me what has happened."

"Now, Lady—"

"Immediately, John!" I hit the bench with my hand, making an unimpressive thud. Ancestors, I was so weak!

"It'll pain you to hear it, and I'm sorry. They were caught in Lady Zella's room. They were trying to hurt her. Poor girl – nearly beside herself with fright, she was. Dreadful."

"What happened to them?" I demanded impatiently.

"Banished, Lady. The king exiled 'em. Course, I weren't there myself, but there was all that commotion up at the Hall, and the next thing we knew there was you and Lady Zella both taken to your beds and the king storming up and down saying that if he ever set eyes on any of your brothers again he'd kill them himself. Can't say as I blame him."

I can, I thought bitterly. Banished his own sons – his own blood. The stupid, blind fool. I bit my lip. They were all right. They *were*. I'd know in my heart if they were gone; know in my flesh and bones. Besides, Father would not have taken the trouble to banish them otherwise. So they were out there somewhere, and if they possibly could, they would find me. It might take time, but they'd search until we were together again. They'd never leave me alone. Never.

"Are you feeling well, Lady? Would you like some of Lady Zella's medicine?"

I blinked and looked at John again. He had taken a stoppered bottle from the basket, and uncorked it as I watched. The bitter scent of half moss and crowberries reached my nose. It was the smell of a powerful sleeping draught, a potion to dull the mind and befuddle the senses.

"Medicine?" I murmured.

"Lady Zella made it for you with her own hands. She gave it to you herself too, even though you didn't wake properly. Ever so concerned for you, she was."

Oh, yes – very concerned. That devious witch. No wonder I was as weak as an invalid. Enough of that potion and I would never have woken. For a fleeting moment I wondered why she hadn't done just that – fed me the stuff until I died. But perhaps she only needed me out of the way for a short while.

"No, John, thank you. I don't need any more medicine," I said absently as he offered me the bottle. What was Zella up to? "Where are we going, John?"

"Didn't I say, Lady? I'm taking you to Midland, to stay with your aunt, your mother's sister."

"Who – what? My *aunt*?"

My mother had hardly ever spoken of her elder sister and I'd certainly never met the woman. Long before I was born she had married a nobleman from the neighbouring kingdom, Midland, and she had never visited her old home.

"Why?" I asked incredulously.

"For you to get better, Lady," said John. "Lady Zella said that you needed peace and quiet to heal, and what with all the hustle and bustle, you'd never get it at the Hall. So the king said he'd send a messenger to your aunt and you could stay there until you were better."

A thought crystallized in my mind. "Hustle and bustle?"

"Yes, getting ready for the wedding."

Ancestors – the wedding! "John, quickly, turn us around."

"Now, don't fuss yourself—"

"John, please, I have to get back before the wedding. It's vital." I *have* to stop it. Somehow I have to stop Father before he marries that woman.

"Well now, I'm sorry but I can't do that."

"John—"

"No, no, Lady, I don't blame you for wanting to be there. But 'tis too late for us to see it now."

"Too late?" I whispered, my blood icing over.

"I'm afraid so, Lady. The wedding was the day before yesterday – the same day that you and I set out. Lady Zella will be our lady by now, all right and proper."

I slumped back against the rough sacking seat.

Too late.

Zella was my father's queen. Now the whole Kingdom would pay the price of my failure. I could do nothing.

I heard John's words of concern distantly and waved them away. "Yes, yes," I muttered. "I am well. Drive on; let us be gone."

As John climbed up behind the horse and we rumbled into motion down the rough track, I turned to look back over the rippling grey-purple grasses. Somewhere beyond these fields and trees lay the Hall. Where Zella now ruled in my mother's place.

I could not return. I no longer had my brothers to protect me and Zella would not have wedding plans to distract her now; she would squash me as easily as a fly. Left to my own devices I was worse than useless. All my hopes rested with David, Robin and Hugh. They would know what to do, how to wrest our home from the grasp of that creature.

Until then, there was nothing to be done. At least in Midland I would be safe.

The next few days passed in a weary blur. I had been through so much in the last few months, suffered so much grief and upheaval, that perhaps my emotions had worn out. Certainly I was unable to sustain such passions now. I felt flat and dull and my only real feeling was to miss my brothers – and that I *did* feel, desperately. I had never been without them before.

It occurred to me, as we rattled along, that this journey was an ill-conceived, hasty affair. A king's daughter was usually afforded more consideration than to be bundled into a rickety trap with no more than half her clothing, untidily packed, and not enough food to last the trip. It was lucky that the land's fruits were easy for me to find and harvest, or we would both have been hungry before long.

Why had I been shunted off with such little notice, only the day before the wedding? Perhaps Zella *had* meant to kill me and had reconsidered at the last moment. The idea of that murderous witch granting mercy to anyone – especially me – was too far-fetched to ring true. I resigned myself to wondering, and was grateful that someone had at least thought to pack bathing oil, so that on the evenings when we stopped by a river I could get properly clean.

Gradually the land began to change. As the lush green hills and fields gave way to dense forest, I began to sense that the currents of enaid were ... not fading, but lessening in strength. They eddied sluggishly between the trees, without the vigorous energy I had always known.

"We're in Midland now, aren't we?" I asked John.

"Indeed, Lady Alexandra. We passed the border about a day back."

I looked around me with interest – the first real feeling I had had in days. When we broke through the dense cover of forest, the land to the west soared away above us, rising abruptly into great yellow-brown hills. Beyond them, more distant peaks were smudged purple and grey against the iron-white sky and topped with raggedy clouds. To the east was rolling moorland, covered in scrubby plants with tiny purple or white flowers that grew twisted into strange shapes and rippled and jumped in the whistling wind. Here and there a jagged boulder or jumble of stones would thrust up out of the froth of plants, startlingly pale against the darkness of the moor.

It was a harsher, fiercer land than my home, and I felt instinctively that it should have been awash with untamed life. But instead of the joyful wildness I expected, there was a sense of weariness and melancholy that echoed my own.

I kneeled up on the front seat so that I could see John's face. "Tell me about Midland," I said.

"Well, now." He clicked his tongue at the horse, and shifted in the seat. "I've not been here often with the king, you understand, trading being what it is. This is a sad land. Good fertile soil, but no one left to till it."

"Why? What happened to the people?"

"War, Lady. They've only been at peace here, oh, thirty years or so. For a more'n hundred before that, there's been nothing but fighting in this place."

"Of course – I remember now. Mama said..." I stopped, composed myself, and began again. "I knew there was a war. It didn't last a hundred years, though."

"The fighting was off and on. But there was never proper peace, I don't think. Too many brothers and cousins and uncles in their ruling family, each one thinking he ought to be the prince. They've all killed each other now; there's only the one left, and he's on the throne, so maybe the peace'll last this time. Land hasn't recovered yet. Too many lost in the fighting; no one left to look after it."

I rested my chin on folded hands – ignoring the teeth-rattling bumps – and stared out over the moor. It was just as Angharad had said. That was why the land felt so sad. It was crying out for want of love.

Slowly our path began to rise. We made our way through more forests and finally began to see signs of human habitation. Tiny crofts and holdings appeared, which gave way to slightly larger houses and settlements in neat fields, though their crops seemed meagre to me. Once or twice we passed others on the road. The people nodded and smiled at us, but they looked thin and tired.

Then, as we emerged through a gap between stony outcroppings, I saw it. Sprawled across the valley floor, it looked like the skeleton of some giant winged creature that had fallen to earth, its highest point rising up to spear the belly of the sky.

"Oh, John," I breathed. "What is that?"

"'Tis the city, Lady. That's where their prince lives now."

"People *live* in it?" I asked incredulously. I stared at the immense grey and white sprawl, trying to make sense of its impossibly tall towers, bright snapping flags and shiny, glassed windows. It must house more people than I had ever seen in my life.

"They don't use a bit of wood and daub, this lot," John said knowledgeably. "Nor thatching neither. Not even for cattle sheds. I call it unnatural, though this city were thought very pretty in its day. They called it the City of Flowers once. But our road don't lay down there. We're heading east now – for the coast."

He turned the trap from the wide paved path onto a smaller track of beaten dirt. My eyes stayed on the city until it disappeared from sight.

We followed the winding path onto the moors, moving slowly downhill now. On our fourth day in Midland, the air changed, slowly becoming sharp with a strange salty tang. I inhaled deeply, trying to think why it smelled so familiar.

"That be the sea, Lady," John said, noticing my intent expression.

I took another deep breath. I *had* smelled it before, I realized – in the darkness of my drugged sleep. But why had that scent come to me then?

Our path began to ascend again, the wild sharp smell

growing stronger; and as we topped a rise, the sea came into view on the horizon. Its great grey-green waves roiled and crashed against the rocks below. I leaned as far as I could over the side of the trap, my hair blowing violently in the wind as I watched water fling itself up and turn silver on the cliffs.

"Careful there!" shouted John above the boom and roar. The trap lurched on the uneven path. "You could fall!"

Reluctantly I eased back, but the savage gales still whipped my cheeks and hair. Too soon the path veered away again, and the sea sank out of view. I sighed. I had never seen anything that looked so much like the currents of enaid that ebbed through the land.

As the sun began to fall down behind the horizon, we rounded a bluff; and there, like a rocky fist thrust out of the land, was my aunt's house.

CHAPTER
SEVEN

It was a hulking three-storey structure, hewn from dark stone, its windows shining in the dying sunlight. The iron-braced door stood several feet taller than a man. At the house's side an enormous dead tree, twisted by the sea winds into a tortured S, tangled its bony white branches with the sky. Not a bird sang; not an animal stirred. The only noise was the susurration of the hidden sea.

John drew the trap to a halt and climbed down, coming round to help me out. My feet touched the ground, but I clutched his hand when he tried to withdraw it.

"John – you will stay a little, won't you?" I asked. "You won't just leave?"

"You won't miss me, Lady, once you've settled. You have family here. They'll look after you."

I stared at the house, unhappily aware that I *would* miss him. I was a stranger in this land, with its wild beauty and sad, tired enaid. He was my last link to my old life, and I did not want to be alone. Then I reminded myself that my brothers were searching for me and they would surely come for me soon. I wasn't alone. I released John's hand and straightened my shoulders.

He smiled reassuringly at me, then went to the door and knocked smartly. After a long moment it swung open to reveal a girl – a few years older than I – dressed in a severe black gown.

"Yes?" she said, face blank.

"Lady Eirian's niece, the Lady Alexandra, has arrived," he said grandly.

The girl cast a doubtful look at me, then looked back at John. "Wait here, please." She shut the door gently in John's face.

I blinked. This was not hospitality as I knew it.

After a few minutes the door reopened.

"Her ladyship will see her niece in the small parlour," the maid said tonelessly. "Please take your ... conveyance to the rear of the building. The footmen will help you unload it."

She stepped back, gesturing for me to precede her. John gave me a nod and an encouraging look. I straightened my back once again and stepped through the door.

The vestibule beyond was dark and narrow, the walls lined with polished wood tables and chests that held dozens of ornaments. Little pottery figurines, vases, glass balls, candlesticks – what light there was gleamed dully on these trinkets as if their purpose was to capture and soak it up. My steps were muffled by a thick, dark red carpet. I moved tentatively, my greatest impression that of stillness. If I screamed or jumped up and down and stamped my feet, would the stillness absorb the noise, so that all anyone would hear would be a faint whirring, like a trapped butterfly's wings?

The corridor ahead branched into three. The maid stepped past me with a quick bob and went to the left-hand branch, opening the first door we came to. I walked into the room she had revealed.

I noticed first the tall thin windows, reaching up to the ceiling. They were swathed with dark curtains so the only light that could penetrate was an eye-smarting hard white line which seemed to go no further than the well of the window itself. The rest of the room was draped in cobwebby shadow that lay over the dim shapes of massive furniture like a physical thing. It was a moment before I even saw the woman in the throne-like chair at the centre of the room. I could make out no more than the hint of finely worked lace at her throat.

I stepped forward hesitantly. The woman lifted her head and I saw her face for the first time. It was all I could do to contain a gasp.

I knew from my mother's rare mentions of her sister

that Eirian had been only two years older. The woman staring at me looked at least two decades older than my mother. Her face was gaunt, marked with deep lines at her eyes and mouth; her lips were a thin, pale line. Her hair was the same red-gold that I knew, softly pulled back into a knot at the nape of her neck, but it was streaked with great bands of white at the temples. Most startling of all to me were her eyes. Instead of the compelling leaf green I had unconsciously expected, they were a pale icy blue – the same colour, I realized with a jolt, as Hugh's. The woman had a startling beauty, but it was like that of the dead tree outside, bleached white and tinged with sorrow.

She looked at me silently; the only change in her expression was the quirk of one fine, beautifully arched brow. Plucked, I thought. Mother's had been straight like mine.

Then she spoke, and it was my mother's voice, exactly as I had last heard it. "So ... you are my sister's daughter." She squinted at me, sending deep lines arrowing up to her forehead. "Disappointing. I expected more. Your features lack fineness. Your figure has no elegance. And your hair... You obviously take after your father."

My teeth snapped together at her rudeness.

"Come closer," she commanded.

I ground my teeth as I obeyed, shocked and angry. How could this woman be my mother's sister? Yet she was. It was undeniable.

She reached out one hand – an ugly, stubby-fingered hand – and grasped my chin. The skin of her fingers was soft and well cared for against my face as she ran her gaze over me. Perhaps she meant to cow me with her disparaging look, but I was too angry to moderate my stare. I met her eyes with the full force of my outrage. She flinched, a tiny sound escaping her. Her hand fell away from me and she covered her face with it, shrinking back into the depths of the seat. Suddenly she seemed small and frail. I was stunned by the strength of her reaction and just starting to feel ashamed of myself, when she spoke again.

"You certainly have her eyes." Her voice was steady, though she continued to hide behind her hand. "More importantly, you have her wildness. I can see it in you. If you try to follow her path, you will have the same end as her – an unfortunate one."

There was a short silence, broken only by the sound of my rapid, angry breaths. How dare this withered, dried-up old woman talk about my mother so? I dared not speak. I was frightened of what I might say.

"While you are in my home," she continued, "you will behave properly, as a young lady should. If I see any signs of your mother's temperament, I will know how to act. You may go now; Anne will take you to your room."

I turned and stalked out. Anne quickly closed the door behind me, and then waited in silence as I stood, shaking with anger and trying to gather my calm again. After a moment, I nodded at her, and she led me back along the corridor to another door, which she opened for me. I went past her into the room. It was small but scrupulously clean, and filled with dark, looming furniture. The mantel and fireplace were tiny and unlit. The bed I did recognize, but it was strange to me – carved of wood and perched on legs, rather than sunken into the floor like the ones at the Hall. Surely you would fall off in the night?

As these thoughts trickled through my mind, the larger part of my attention was fixed on the small glassed window opposite me. It looked out over a large square of closely trimmed yellowing grass, edged with sad rose bushes that were all thorn and no flower. Beyond was a pale, tussocky hump of land with what looked like a deer trail leading over it. The way to the sea? I fumbled with the unfamiliar latch, trying to open the window and let the air in.

"'Tis no use, Lady," Anne said quietly from behind me. "The mistress had it nailed up."

I turned to stare at her. "Why?"

Her gaze did not lift from her toes. "I couldn't say, Lady." She wrung her hands. Suddenly I heard what she could not say. It had been shut up to keep me in. That realization was the final straw. Overwhelmed by weariness, I sat down on the strange bed with a bump and put my head in my hands. What was I doing here?

I had forgotten that Anne was in the room until a hand came to rest tentatively on my shoulder. "There now, Lady," she whispered. "Don't take on so."

I raised my head to look at her, and saw kindness – perhaps even pity – in her eyes.

"She doesn't even know me,"

I whispered back. "Why should she hate me so?"

"She doesn't. Don't think that, Lady. The mistress is, well ... difficult."

The moment the words left her mouth I could tell she regretted them. Looking shocked at herself, she straightened and removed her hand.

"I ... Mistress said you should have your supper in here, Lady. I'll bring it to you in a few minutes, then I'll draw your bath and unpack for you." She bobbed a quick curtsy, and hurried out of the room.

I put my head back in my hands. As I sat there in the faded bluish light, I realized that I had said not a word during my interview with my aunt. I'd let her silence me, just as my father always had. Why could I never speak up for myself?

Please come for me soon, I begged my brothers silently. Robin, David, Hugh...please come soon.

Supper was a plain affair. I was offered something called tea – bitter brown liquid that I could not stomach. I drank milk instead, but found it watery. There was a flan, a round pastry base filled with egg, onion, tomatoes and mushrooms, and there were boiled potatoes with butter. I refused the cooked chicken and ate instead the mashed-up mixture of carrot and swede with more butter. I finished with a strange pudding, which mostly consisted of bread soaked in milk, though there seemed to be some fruit in it too. I was puzzled by the lack of flavour in everything I ate. Even the tomatoes, usually a favourite of mine, were almost tasteless. I was offered salt – a rare delicacy at home – but I found that once I sprinkled it on the food, it was all I could taste.

The bath, at least, was a comfort. My mother had made Father purchase copper bathing tubs from Midland when I was very young, so the gleaming metal bath that was placed before the now blazing fire was familiar and welcome.

By the time I emerged, pink with scrubbing and the heat, I was so sleepy that it was all I could do to keep my eyes open as the maid towelled my hair dry. Before the footmen came to take the bath away from the hearth, I had fallen into bed and into sleep.

As far back as I could remember, the tides of enaid had filled my dreams. I felt them wash and ebb in a way that was more than hearing or seeing; they rippled through my own veins, or perhaps carried me with them like a leaf swept along with the rush of a river. They had lulled me to sleep from the cradle.

During that first night at my aunt's house, they were

not enough. The weak whispering of magic in this country was too fraint to drown out the unfamiliar noises of the house settling around me. I woke in the darkness, and could not find sleep again. I had dreamed of those pale things that had flown through my tortured mind the night my brothers and I crept into Zella's room. They were the rare great white swans, I realized, mute swans. Their shadows had passed over me in my dream, and I had looked up to see them, their wings rippling and spreading across the sky like clouds, their wing beats like thunder.

Gradually, as sleep faded, I became aware that the thundering noise was not all in my dream. It was the sound of the sea. It seemed to roar against the closed window. Surely it had not been so loud before. Maybe the tide of water was coming in, just as the tides of magic had done at home. The thought of home made me clench my eyes shut. I would see my home again. I just had to wait.

I flung the sheets back and climbed out of the detestable bed to go to the window. I laid my hands on the wooden sill and felt through it with my mind for the metal nails. They would have to come out.

I had harboured a secret fear that in this magic-starved land my skills might not work, but it was as easy as ever to call on them. I let my awareness trickle down through my feet into the earth and out through my hands into the air. There was a surprisingly strong surge of power in response, and I used it to ask the wood to expel the intrusion of metal from its body. The sill contracted and wriggled slightly under my touch, like a sleeping cat woken with a stroke to its back, and then the nails fell to the floor with a quiet plink. I pushed the window open.

Clean, tangy air rushed in as though it had been clamouring to enter. I looked out. The darkness was no problem to me – I had always had cat's eyes – and I looked at the hump of land with its intriguing path, and the thin golden moon embedded in the sky above. I hitched up the trailing skirt of my nightgown and sat on the sill, then slipped over it and down to the ground.

Beneath my feet the grass was so short that it felt like moss, cool and soft. My toes curled into it as I turned to look up at the shadowy house towering behind me, and thanked the Ancestors that I had been given a room on the ground floor. Above, the sky was dotted with frosty points of light – the same stars I had always known. I was not so far from home.

My bare feet made no noise on the grass as I set off, skirting the house and the rose bushes until I came to a wrought-iron fence. Luckily the gate was unlocked; and beyond it, like entering a different world, I stepped into olio grass, its greyish-pink feathery fronds dancing almost as high as my head, tiny white lister flowers blooming among them. I felt the tension begin to fade from my body as I looked around me.

The earth beneath my feet was pale and crumbly, more sand than soil. I saw the deer trail ahead, and climbed through the grasses towards it, moving up the gentle hill I had seen from my window. Others might have found this bare foot progress painful, but my soles were as tough as leather, and I was more sure-footed without shoes. The sounds of the tide grew louder as the land rose, beckoning me on.

I reached the top of the hill and saw the white band of the shore and the surging, seething expanse of the sea. Moonlight glinted over the rippling water, silvering intricate patterns of foam on the waves' surface. It was beautiful. This was a good place. I went down the dune at a half-run, kicking up little explosions of sand. When I reached the bottom I sat down to watch the changing face of the water, oblivious of the state of my nightgown.

The rolling and sighing of the waves was almost hypnotic. My mind emptied, and I relaxed completely for the first time since reaching this place, savouring the breeze that gently lifted and stroked my hair. After a few more moments, I stood and went to the edge of the water, where the sea music drowned out all other sounds. I let out a shocked laugh as the cold water broke over my feet and soaked the hem of my gown. I jumped and twirled in the foam, my nightdress flying up above my knees in the wind.

I might have danced there for hours, thinking myself alone. It was only when I spun a full circle that I saw the man.

He stood watching me, only a few feet away, just far enough that the surf would not soak his fine leather boots. He was very tall, and his dark hair drifted in the wind like the long cloak clasped at his shoulder with a silver brooch.

Strangely my first reaction was not fear, but self-consciousness that I had been caught playing in the sea in my nightgown with my hair a tangled mess. In my surprise I took a step away, and then toppled backwards as the sand disintegrated under my heel. I would have landed in the water, but he took two swift steps forward and caught me, then pulled me out of the waves up onto the beach.

"Oh – thank you! I'm sorry," I babbled, looking down at the now soaked leather of his boots with dismay.

He ignored my words but held on to my arms, his eyes searching my face with what looked like astonishment.

"You're real," he muttered, as if to himself.

"What? Of course I'm real." I pulled away, embarrassed by my own clumsiness, his strange expression, and by the fine clothes that showed he was an important person. I was a king's daughter – I shouldn't be meeting people in a wet nightgown with draggled hair.

The odd look disappeared from his face as he released me, and he let out a quiet laugh.

"There's no 'of course' about it," he said. "I saw you as I came down the beach, dancing in the waves with your hair all flying – I thought you were a selkie or a mermaid."

I avoided his amused grey eyes, and looked down at my grubby toes in the sand. "Well, I'm not."

There was a moment of silence – if silence it could be called, with the rush and sigh of the water – and then he asked, "Do you live here? My family come here every year, but I've never seen you before."

"No, I'm only here for a little while. I'm staying with my aunt, up there." I pointed to where the peak of the house could be seen. "I've just arrived." I risked another look at his face. He was only a few years older than me – seventeen, perhaps. "Aren't you going to ask me what I'm doing out here at this time of night?"

"The same thing as me, I imagine." He smiled. "Trying to think – or to stop thinking. Here." He reached up to unclasp the silver brooch at his shoulder and then held his cloak out to me. "You're wet; you must be cold."

On the verge of refusing, I looked up and caught his eye. The silvery colour of his gaze held my attention. Like storm clouds, I thought absently. He smiled again, and pushed the soft weight of the cloak into my hands.

"Don't look so stunned," he said. "It's only a cloak."

I took it from him, my eyes still riveted to his, barely aware of my actions.

The look on his face changed again, to concern. "Are you all right?" He broke my stare with no sign of difficulty and took back the cloak to wrap it round my shoulders. "You're shivering. Come and sit out of this wind." He led me to the shelter of a low dune, and made me sit down. "There. Better now?" he asked.

"Yes, thank you. I'm sorry. I'm, er ... a little tired; I've travelled a long way."

He looked relieved. "Good. For a moment I thought you might faint. Look, it's cold. Stay there for a minute while I fetch some driftwood."

I started to say that I had never fainted in my life, but he'd turned away. By the time he came back with a little pile of silvery driftwood and a handful of dry grass, I'd remembered that I had fainted - once.

He sat down opposite me and heaped up the wood and kindling between us. I expected him to pull out a tinderbox, though why he would have brought one on a night walk along the beach I didn't know, but instead he held his hand palm down over the fuel and closed his eyes. I felt a swirl in the enaid around me as it came to attention, and then the wood burst into flame. I gasped in amazement.

"I didn't know boys could do workings!" I blurted, too shocked to think about my words.

He glanced up, the firelight painting rosy patterns on his face and gilding his hair. I thought he was a little embarrassed. "Yes. It's quite rare, I know. I get it from my mother. I can only do little things like this." He looked at me with interest. "Can you do any?" he asked.

"Only small ones," I said, still surprised. "Charming animals and that sort of thing."

"Really?" He grinned conspiratorially. "That's my favourite. I've got our hunting dogs beautifully trained – the hunting master doesn't know if he should love me or hate me."

"Why should he hate you?" I asked curiously, brushing back a hank of hair that had fallen into my eyes.

"Oh, because he liked to make out that training them was so difficult and get heaped with praise for doing such a good job. Now he's got the best dogs in the country, but he can't take the credit for them."

"Oh dear." I couldn't help laughing a little. "I knew someone like that. She used to be famous for making up this wonderful tisane for bad throats, but she kept the recipe a great secret and wouldn't tell me. So I worked it out for myself and found that it was incredibly simple really, and told everyone else. She was furious. It's still called Edie Finch's tisane, though."

He looked at me with respect. "Are you a cunning woman?"

"Not a very good one." I ducked my head, embarrassed as I realized how close I had come to boasting.

"You sound like a good one to me," he said.

I shook my head, not looking up from my hands, which I was warming by the fire.

"Please don't be too modest," he said. "You'll make me feel I was bragging!"

I looked up, unable to stop myself smiling again. "Sorry. But I'm really not much good." The smile died from my face. I shook my head, as if the movement could banish the memories, and asked, "What's your name?"

"Gabriel. And yours? Are you here with your family?"

"I'm Alexandra. And ... no. I left them at home. There's just my aunt." I looked away from him.

He asked, "Where is your home?"

I continued to watch the sea. "I ... Farland, I think you would call it?" I answered.

"Ah." He seized on the topic gratefully. "I thought there was something unusual in your accent. My father calls Farland a wondrous place. He says that the harvests never fail there." He sighed. "I wish that were true of this country."

"The Kingdom is a beautiful place," I said carefully. "But it might not remain so. The king has married an awful woman, and now things will not be the same there for much longer."

He frowned. "I thought the queen of Farland was a famous wise woman."

"She was. She died," I said shortly, willing my voice not to break. "Three months ago."

"And the king has already remarried? We had not heard of it," he said, puzzled.

"You'll hear of it soon enough," I said. "He is besotted with his new queen. He will wish their marriage to be celebrated far and wide."

Gabriel said carefully, "You do not believe his choice is wise, then?"

"No. Not wise at all." Now I sighed.

There was another pause, but a friendly one, filled with the night sea noises.

Then he asked, "I don't suppose you know anything about the farms?"

"Farms?" I looked at him in surprise and was again caught by the dark silver of his eyes.

"Yes. They're the pride of Farland, aren't they? And the farmers use special methods to make the land fertile. Do you know anything about them?"

I studied his face, and then the strength of his hands where they lay on the sand. I remembered the sadness in his voice when he wished his country shared the fertility of the Kingdom.

He loved this land. He loved Midland as much as I loved the Kingdom.

I began to talk. I explained the special system of crop rotation and fallow land, the planting of certain herbs that discouraged pests, the grinding of minerals and fish bones to add to manure. All these things my mother had taught me; many had been her own inventions. Gabriel's knowledgeable questions added to my liking. He obviously knew a lot about farming and was keen to learn more; nor, his comments revealed, did he think physical labour beneath him like some men who wore fine clothes.

After a while our conversation wandered away again and we spoke on many different subjects, most of which I cannot remember now. I learned that there was a little town, about a mile along the coast, just out of sight. His family came each year at the end of summer to take the sea air.

In return I told him guiltily edited stories of my own home. How could I say that my mother had been Lady Branwen the Wise? Ladies were not supposed to sit on the sand in their nightclothes and talk with strangers. Nor did I wish to speak of the horrors that had overtaken me so recently; I didn't even want to think about them.

How long we sat on the shore I do not know, but when I glanced up I saw the milky wash of light in the west that drowned out the stars, and knew it was near dawn.

"I didn't notice the night go. It's almost morning," he said, surprised, as he followed my gaze.

"Yes." I scrambled up, pulling the heavy cloak from my shoulders. The servants would be up soon, and I did not want to think of the fuss it would cause if my bed was found empty. "I must go now," I said, giving the woollen bundle to him as he rose.

"So must I," he said ruefully. "Um ... would you like to meet me here again? Tomorrow?"

I smiled, realizing how much I had enjoyed the past few hours. It had almost been like speaking to one of my brothers – though none of their eyes mesmerized as me at his did. "When?"

"An hour after sunfall. Can you get away then?"

"Yes. I'll be here." I didn't question our shared desire to keep our meetings secret.

With another look at the lightening sky, I turned to run up the bank of sand.

"Goodbye!" He waved at me as I reached the top of the dune. I waved too, then went back along the path as quickly as I could.

A few minutes later I was through the window, closing it tightly behind me, and slipping into bed. Perhaps it was the sea air, but this time when I closed my eyes the sleep that claimed me was a peaceful one, and I did not dream, except of the sighing tide.

CHAPTER
EIGHT

It was lucky for me that my aunt's household did not keep the same hours I was used to. Instead of being woken by the activity of my family an hour or so after dawn, I slept until mid-morning and was gently roused by Anne. She had brought me warm milk – having kindly remembered my dislike of tea – in a fine, thin cup that I hardly dared grip for fear it would crack under my fingers. I drank the watery stuff so as not to offend her, and watched sleepily as she bustled around the room.

I took no notice of what she was doing as she bent down near the window, until I heard her mutter, "These floors ... muck everywhere..."

I stiffened, my fingers tightening on the precious cup. Anne was staring at the floor at swirls of sand on the carpet. Sand I had trailed in last night. I saw her eyes go to the window and then back to the sand beneath it, heard her small inhalation of breath. We were both frozen, still as statues, me staring at Anne, Anne staring at the sand.

But perhaps that stirring of pity I had seen in her before intervened, for she straightened without another word, and within a few moments had quietly and efficiently swept away the dirt. Nor did she blink at the state of my nightgown or the sheets, merely took them away and replaced them with clean new ones. Her avoidance of my eye was the lone indicator that she had noticed anything unusual.

When I had risen and washed, she took one of my newer dresses from the tall box against the wall – the wardrobe – and helped me to dress, though I had been able to put on and lace my own gowns for many years. But I baulked when she tried to pin up my hair; I had always worn it loose, and besides felt the need of something to hide behind. She gave in with a sigh of dissatisfaction.

The reason for the special attention became clear when she led me out into the passage again.

"The mistress usually has breakfast in her room, but today you are to breakfast together in the upper parlour."

I followed her along the shadowy corridor and up some cramped stairs, waiting for the sense of oppression to settle over me but today I felt less cowed, brighter. The heaviness did not affect me as it had yesterday. Nor did I worry overmuch about the meeting with my aunt. Somehow I had found freedom in the night along with my new friend. My aunt owned this house, but she did not own me.

The upper parlour was on the second floor of the house, and I was surprised to find it a bright room, full of sunlight that streamed, butter yellow, through the windows despite the dark walls and furniture. It was dominated by a long table, as shiny as a mirror. My aunt sat at the furthest end, pale and still in a dark blue gown. I jumped when a man materialized out of the wall, to seat me opposite my aunt and serve my breakfast. This house seemed to muffle my natural awareness of others, the walls soaking up noise and energy as sheep's wool absorbs water.

The dark-garbed man brought me a fine plate and poured milk into a cup. Anne had obviously spoken to him. I wondered if I would be forced to drink nothing but milk for the duration of my stay. Perhaps I should ask Anne about apple juice. I looked with trepidation at the food I had been given. At home the morning meal was usually porridge with honey, or potato cakes fried in butter. On my plate now were eggs, which had been whipped up in some way and made fluffy, and several triangle-shaped pieces of what seemed to be singed bread, with butter. Mercifully no meat – probably Anne again. The man bowed to me, then to Aunt Eirian, and silently departed. Only then did my aunt look at me.

"Good morning, Alexandra."

I looked back at her – or rather, at the point just above her left shoulder – as I responded formally, "Good morning, Aunt."

Her teacup clinked gently as she placed it in the saucer.

There was silence as I dubiously tasted the fluffy eggs and found them tolerable.

"How old are you?" she asked abruptly.

I kept my eyes on the plate. "I am fifteen."

"You look older." There was another moment of quiet. "But no matter. Your clothes are dreadful. I have sent for my personal dressmaker from the village; she will outfit you appropriately."

My fingers tightened on my knife and fork, but I held my tongue. It wasn't important. If she wanted to waste her gold on clothes, I could hardly stay her; I would simply leave them behind when my brothers came.

"And that hair ... it will have to be cut."

Now I did look up. Her tone had not been bland enough to disguise the faint tinge of satisfaction at the idea. What possible happiness cutting off my hair would give her, I did not know – but I did know that I wouldn't allow it to happen. Mama had loved my hair.

I let my eyes rest on her face, and saw her jaw clench.

"No." I was startled by the calmness of the word. I didn't feel calm – I could feel my heart speeding. But my voice was steady, and so were my hands as I scooped up another bite of egg.

"I beg your pardon?" Her voice was as cold as cracking ice.

I shifted my gaze again, allowing my eyes to meet hers for a split second, no more, before I returned it to the eggs.

"My hair will stay as it is."

There was a long, terrible pause, in which the silence purred ominously. When Eirian's voice finally came, it was quiet and surprisingly shaky.

"You will allow us to plait and pin it."

I thought about it. There was no reason to argue. Pins and braiding were not permanent. But I didn't believe she had admitted defeat – nor did I want her to think that I would take orders from her. In the end, I only sighed. "Perhaps."

I was glad of the tiny noises that eating made. I had never met such suffocating silence as that which filled this house.

Eirian reached one small white hand out and picked up a little silver bell that sat at her elbow. The quiet tinkle had barely pierced the quiet when the dark-suited man appeared again. I watched in silence as he drew back her chair and helped her out of it. Her gait was stiff and awkward; she leaned heavily on his arm, her free hand clutching a silver-topped cane which made soft thudding noises on the carpet as she passed me.

I looked away, made uncomfortable by this evidence of weakness, though I sensed no emotion from her about it. At the door she paused, saying nothing, until I looked up.

"I will call for you when the seamstress arrives. Anne will take you back to your room." She kept her eyes on my collar as she spoke, then turned and limped slowly down the corridor.

I looked down at my plate, somehow ashamed, though I was unsure why. My aunt was bitter and unkind, yet her will had bent before me. This morning she had seemed almost frightened of me. I shook my head, trying to dislodge the complicated thoughts. None of it mattered anyway. I wouldn't be here long.

I put my knife and fork down, and stood, pushing the chair back myself. I could find my own way to my room; I might as well learn to find my way about while I was here. I opened the heavy door and went into the corridor.

I spent a little time exploring the house, but despite the abundance of trinkets and baubles that littered every available surface, there was not much of interest. Every room was so stuffed with things that the eye soon tired of searching through them. I wandered aimlessly about, building a map of the house in my head; but finally, bored, I returned to my room. I almost expected to find Anne there waiting for me, but the room was as empty and tranquil as I had left it.

I crossed to the window and looked at the faint line of the path disappearing into the grasses. My eyes followed it longingly but I suppressed the urge to throw up the window and escape into the fresh air again. Anne would come for me soon. And anyway, Gabriel wouldn't be there until tonight.

So I sat on the bed to wait. I wondered what had happened to John. I hoped my aunt's servants had treated him well, and that he would come to see me before he left. Despite his susceptibility to the devious witch and his hostility towards my brothers, I had grown fond of him on our journey. He was a good man. I let my thoughts dwell on him because otherwise they might return home. To Zella and my father and all the other thoughts that made me feel cold and frightened.

It wasn't long before I heard the quiet knock at the door. As I left the room I asked Anne, "Has John been looked after?"

"Your groom, Lady? He slept well in the kitchen last night and ate a good breakfast before he left this morning."

"Left? He's gone?"

"Yes, Lady. At first light. He was anxious to get home."

I sighed. Well, what had I expected? He had discharged his obligation to bring me safely here, and he was just as much under Zella's spell as anyone in the Household.

"Lady?"

"Oh, I beg your pardon, Anne." I realized I had been stood silently for too long, and began to move again.

The session with my aunt's plump dressmaker was long and very tedious. My aunt sat in another of her throne-like chairs, issuing orders while they more or less ignored me. The dressmaker measured and remeasured me and pinned pieces of fabric to my limbs and torso. My aunt's voice droned on. The patterns must be plain, even severe. No lace or ornamentation. Some muslin, silk, and wool, of course – at least one good velvet. The materials must be dark. Dove grey, black, deep blue at the very brightest. She waved away the village woman's suggestion of any green or white.

"My niece," she said grandly, "is in mourning."

I stood through it uncomplainingly, but as soon as the last sleeve was unpinned I fled, and vowed never to put up with such nonsense again.

That evening, after an almost silent meal with my aunt, I threw open the bedroom window again and climbed out into the garden. I made my way eagerly through the tall whispering grasses along the dunes and down to the sea.

The sea was far away tonight, lying around the headland like a giant sleeping creature. Gabriel was nowhere to be seen, so I stood with my bare toes curling in the slowly drying sand and watched the sun fall alone. The horizon was heaped with clouds, their drifting underbellies snowy white. For a split second I thought I could make out shapes in those clouds, like pale birds in flight...

I sensed Gabriel's arrival at my shoulder but neither of us spoke until the last flicker of sunlight had been doused in the sea, and the sky darkened to twilight. I sighed as I turned to look at him. His expression held traces of the same awe and melancholy I felt.

"I wonder what lies beyond the sea," he said quietly. "Does it all end where the sun goes down? Or could there be other lands and other people there?"

"My mother taught me that birds – wild geese and swans – migrate over the ocean when the winter snows come, and fly back again in the spring," I said, smiling. "So there must be something out there, where the sun sets. The place where wild swans fly."

He smiled back, and reached out to take my hand. "Come on," he said, his cheerful tone banishing sadness as he tugged me towards the cliff. "I've found a rock pool I want to show you. There's some creatures in it that I want to see if I can charm."

We explored together until yawns punctured our conversation so badly we could no longer speak, and parted with the promise of meeting again the following night.

Each morning I breakfasted with my aunt – though usually neither of us spoke above two words – and then wandered around the house, seeing no one but servants, who always hurried away, until supper. In the evening I would climb out of the window and run down to the sea to meet Gabriel. There I would stay until dawn. The sleepiness this caused made the uneventful days easier to cope with and I was doubly grateful to Gabriel for that.

I think I would have gone mad in those first weeks without him. No matter how bored or lonely I felt in the day, my nights were alive. When I was with him, there was laughter, exhilaration ... joy. If I sometimes felt a twinge of guilt about the strength of the happiness Gabriel made me feel, when by rights I should have been worrying day and night for my brothers, I pushed it down. Why shouldn't I value this unexpected gift of friendship? It was all I had; Gabriel was all I had.

He was ... everything.

Unfortunately, I couldn't spend all my time with him. So I tried to make myself more comfortable in my aunt's home. The one room I was fond of was the library, at the very top of the house. It had a window seat overlooking the sea, and the quiet there seemed peaceful rather than dead. Though the room was meticulously dusted, I was sure that no one but me ever used it, so I decided to make it properly mine. One wall of the room was covered from ceiling to floor with books, and I started at the top left-hand corner and began reading every book there, intending to work my way through the whole lot. In the periods when reading bored me I practised the balancing tricks and tumbling that my brothers had taught me, or performed small workings like changing the colour of the carpets, or charming spiders from nooks and crannies. I reported my success and my failures – like the time all the spiders ended up hiding in my hair – to Gabriel, and we laughed about them together. Thinking of new ways to make him laugh became my main occupation in life.

The weeks passed slowly, but they did pass, and every day, I was sure, brought my brothers closer to me.

One evening I went to meet Gabriel on the beach as normal, with a story from one of my books to tell him. But though he listened with interest, his usual enthusiasm was missing.

"What's wrong?" I asked him eventually. I saw hesitation in his face and urged, "Please tell me."

He traced a pattern in the sand with his finger, and then looked at me, his eyes unhappy. "How long do you think you will stay here?"

I was startled by the question and blinked at him. "I – I don't know." It couldn't be much longer, could it? I had been here ... Ancestors, over two months now. My brothers would be on their way. "Not long. Why?" I finished enquiringly.

"My father's affairs need his attention. I think we will have to leave soon." He shrugged. "Normally we stay longer."

"But—" I stopped myself before I could say more. He had to leave sooner or later. So did I. I'd always known that.

He met my eyes again. "I think we may stay a few days more – a week even. But when we go we will not be able to return until next year, spring at the earliest."

"Spring?" The word leaped from my lips, but again I could not continue. It didn't matter. It didn't. I would be gone soon anyway. I looked away from him. Don't you dare cry, Alexandra!

I cleared my throat and said, "I thought your family only came here for the summer."

"I can persuade my father to bring us back early. In the autumn and winter we are needed. But we will be able to return in the spring." He paused. We both looked away.

Then he grabbed my hands. My fingers curled tightly around his as he asked, "Alexandra, do you think you will be here in the spring?"

I took a deep breath, ashamed of the way it shuddered in my chest. "No. I don't think so." I could not wish it otherwise. I did not wish it otherwise.

"But if you are still here then, will you meet me? At the first new moon after the thaw?"

I closed my eyes. It's stupid to make promises. I'll be gone by then.

Then I felt the warmth of his breath on my face and the moistness of his mouth pressed against mine. I gasped a little in surprise, and as my lips parted his did too – and suddenly I was kissing him back, clutching at him as his fingers buried themselves in the heavy curls of my hair.

"Alexandra..." he said as he eased back. His breath was ragged, and there was despair in his voice. "Promise me. Promise you'll meet me after the thaw."

I leaned weakly against his shoulder, blinking to dry my eyes. You won't be here. He's lying to himself. You're lying to each other. You won't be here.

Finally I lifted my head to meet his gaze. "I promise," I whispered. "If ... I can, I will meet you."

His face lit with a smile that made my heart pulse wildly, and he kissed me again. I was breathing hard when he let me go, but I tried once more to prepare him. "Gabriel, if I am not here—"

"Then I will know that you have returned home and ... and I will be happy for you." He finished rapidly as though the words were painful, rising to his feet and pulling me with him. "Don't worry. Come on – it'll be too dark to walk soon."

I went with him, trying to convince myself that it would be all right. Gabriel would have long forgotten me by spring anyway. It would all be for the best.

My brothers would be here soon.

PART TWO

CHAPTER NINE

It was a long time before I admitted to myself that my brothers were not coming for me.

I think I had always known it, somewhere inside – known that Zella's malevolence could not be so easily shrugged off. Although there were things about that night which I could not remember, I knew that something terrible must have happened. Why would my memories have been so blurred, otherwise? Perhaps then, in those first days following the loss of all I had known, I had needed hope more than truth. We all do, at times.

Gabriel left. The weeks passed into months, late summer became autumn and autumn slipped away into winter. Snow fell; I outgrew my clothes and the seamstress had to be called in again. And still they did not come. The cold of that winter was more bitter than any I had known at home. For much of the time I was confined to the house. I did not have the comfort of the earth under my feet. All I could do was sit on what I had come to think of as my window seat and watch the world freeze into white.

The hard, colourless days passed slowly. I grew adept at twisting and pinning up the long curls of my hair, until I no longer needed Anne's help. I grew used to the weight of the petticoats that my aunt deemed necessary. I began to find taste in even the blandest of the foods presented to me. I worked my way through half of the library and managed a faultless backflip. Still they did not come.

And so, slowly, I sank.

It was black hopelessness, a kind of numb despair, that waited to claim me. I was swallowed up until I seemed to lose myself in it. I can only describe this feeling as something like the shock that can overtake the body in the wake of a serious injury and which can be fatal in its own right. Too much loss had injured my mind and heart. Without a friend to talk to, and with weeks passing without my exchanging more conversation than "please" and "thank you" with the servants – everything turned inwards. I succumbed.

Day after day, I sat on the window seat overlooking the frozen garden, alone. In my mind I dwelled on each separate pain until those memories seemed to engulf me. My mother's death. My father's betrayal. My failure to protect my family. My brothers' disappearance. Though I was still convinced that David, Robin and Hugh were alive, I could no longer fool myself that they would arrive at any moment to rescue me. What would they rescue me from? For all I knew they were worse off than I. With my face pressed against the icy cold of the window, I cried my last tears for my family, and the life I had left behind.

I grew used to stillness and solitude that winter. Eventually, as the new shoots braved the frost, something descended on me – if not contentment, then at least acceptance. The very helplessness that bound me also brought me something like peace. At length, despair relinquished its hold. I tucked away memories of home and my brothers; instead I thought of Gabriel, and looked forward to the thaw and the first new moon. My feelings were echoed by the slow change I had felt in the land as the end of winter approached. With the rising of sap came a surge of new life – the lethargic currents of natural energy gathered strength from some unknown source until they seemed to swirl and well around the house. Perhaps the country was at last recovering from the devastation of war.

As the strength of the enaid grew, so did my own.

One day I wrapped up warmly against the chill of the wind and went out to walk in the garden. I had wandered about alone for some minutes, when I heard a noise behind me and turned to see, most unexpectedly, Aunt Eirian leaving the house. I stared at her as she stumped awkwardly across the grass towards me.

"Good day," she said stiffly.

"Good day, Aunt," I replied with equal graciousness, wishing she would go back in and leave me alone.

"I ... I am glad to see you looking better." She looked away from me, uncomfortable.

"I don't know what you mean," I said coldly.

"Don't take that tone with me," she snapped, abandoning her attempt at manners. "I'm not such a fool that I don't recognize despair when I see it."

I stared at her again, wordless. She tapped her fingernails against the silver top of her walking stick.

"Let me tell you a story, Alexandra. Once there were two sisters. The eldest was a skilled cunning woman, and thought very lovely. At an early age she was betrothed to a young man who was the heir to the throne. This older sister thought herself very lucky, because she truly loved the man she was to marry, and believed he cared for her too. Unbeknown to her, the man she was betrothed to was actually falling in love with her younger sister, who was more beautiful still, and acknowledged as a great wise woman. And the younger sister encouraged this, because she believed that with her greater powers she would do more good as the queen. Eventually the young king broke his engagement and married the younger sister instead. The discarded girl thought that her heart was broken. She couldn't stand to see her sister any more, or the man she had loved; but she had nowhere else to go. She thought it would drive her mad to see them both day after day, to pretend that she did not care when really she wanted to die. Eventually she eloped with a lord of Midland, hoping to escape the pain and humiliation. But her bitterness over the betrayal turned all her strengths – her patience, and her intelligence – inward, twisted and broke them, so that she could never be happy. Her healing gifts went so wrong that she was unable even to heal herself when she was badly hurt in the carriage accident that killed her poor husband. And her new home became barren and cold, and the roses never bloomed there." She sighed. "So you see, I know much of despair."

"I..." I stopped and swallowed, unable to go on. I felt sick and cold – and yet ... I never doubted that what she had said was true. In my heart, I knew that my parents were both capable of what she had said. Hadn't Mother always talked to me of the good of the land? Hadn't she always put that duty before her husband – and even her children? And hadn't my father displayed his faithless, fickle nature in his behaviour after Mother's death?

No, I knew every word was true. I felt a sharp stab of pity and sorrow that I did not know how to express. I began again, and said the only thing I could. "I'm sorry." I looked down at her twisted leg, and then back up into her beautiful, bitter face. "I wish—"

Her face hardened and she shook her head fiercely, cutting me off. "If wishes were horses, beggars would ride."

Then she reached out – for the first time since the day I arrived at her house – and touched me. Her thin fingers felt like twigs; they gripped my shoulder briefly. Then she withdrew them and turned away, stumping back to the house without another word.

As I gazed thoughtfully at the garden, I saw something which had not been there moments ago. It was a fresh, pale green bud on the thorny bush to my left.

A rose would bloom in my aunt's garden this spring.

A week later – only two days before the first full moon of the thaw, when I would meet Gabriel again and also celebrate my sixteenth birthday – I sat in the library, staring out over the dunes to the sea.

It seemed like only a few days since I had spoken to him, but at the same time, an age. I wondered what he had done while he was gone. Read books, and experimented with new workings, perhaps. Trained his dogs and his horses. Ridden out to hunt in the daytime, and gone to parties at night. I tried to imagine his home, but he had hardly ever spoken of details, and I could not make the image clear.

What was he doing right now? I closed my eyes and pictured him in my mind. His eyes that bright, deep silver, and his hair untidily ruffled. I recalled the echo of his laughter, and saw him ... dancing perhaps, with a tall red-haired girl who pressed her face into his neck, and smiled...

I was jolted from these thoughts by the sound of the door opening. I looked up to see Anne enter.

"Lady, your aunt sent me to fetch you. You're to go to the yellow salon. There's people come, from your home."

"People ... yellow salon?" I repeated blankly.

I did not hear another word that Anne said. My heart thundered too loudly. All the hopes and dreams I thought I had banished came rushing back. People from home? My brothers — it must be them! I lifted my heavy skirts and ran past Anne, my kid slippers pattering softly as I flew down the stairs and along the corridors until I reached the yellow salon and pushed open the door.

My aunt turned to look at me as I entered. Her face was as blank as ever, but something in it stopped me dead. For a second my vision seemed to cloud over with darting silver swirls, like the times when I'd stood up too quickly and the blood had rushed to my head. I felt dizzy. Then my spine stiffened until I stood as straight and still as she had taught me. My skirts dropped from my fingers to hang in their proper folds around my feet. I could feel my face going as blank as hers. And deep inside me the hopes that had burst into bloom so briefly withered and died. My brothers were not here. I knew it. She would not look at me so if they were.

She gave a tiny nod, perhaps of approval, and then

turned back to look at the two people sat opposite her. "Is it not the custom to rise when a lady enters the room?" she asked frigidly.

The two people – a man and a woman – hurriedly got to their feet. The man bowed deeply, the woman executed a curtsy, but their eyes stayed on me as if they could barely believe what they saw.

I inclined my head slightly, and they stood politely until I had walked, ever so slowly, across the room to take the seat which had been placed next to my aunt's. Then they sat again, still staring at me. Neither of their faces seemed familiar at first; then I realized that the man was not a complete stranger to me. He had been an occasional hunting companion of my fathers. I had probably spoken no more than a word to him in my life. The woman I was sure I did not know. Why on earth had these two travelled all the way from the Kingdom to see me? What news could they possibly bring?

There was a lengthty silence, during which I allowed myself to examine them as they were doing me. They were both dressed finely, with a great deal of winking gold and silver embroidery that looked rather gaudy beside the restrained elegance of my own and my aunt's clothing. Since when did the household people wear such ostentatious clothing? I had certainly never worn gold thread on my gowns.

"We beg leave to address the Lady Alexandra," the woman said.

I blinked at being addressed with such reverence — why did she stare at me so? — but nodded as regally as I was able.

"I am Isolde of the Hall, one of Lady Zella's women. This is Rother of Westfield, with whom you are already acquainted—"

The man interrupted pompously. "We are come from your esteemed stepmother, Lady Zella, and your father. They have missed you sorely in your absence, Lady."

I gave him a hard look — I was not oblivious to the precedence he had given my stepmother. He fidgeted and avoided my gaze.

The woman's eyes had shifted from my face and were now fixed firmly on my feet. "Your parents require your presence, Lady Alexandra. We have been sent to escort you home."

I stiffened. Beside me, my aunt seemed to straighten too. "I wonder," she said, with quiet ice, "that no one had the courtesy to give us some leave of this sudden change. But then, considering the circumstances of my niece's arrival, perhaps we should be grateful that at least this time she is not to be escorted by a stable hand in a rattle-trap wagon."

There was a moment of silence. The pair shifted in their seats and exchanged glances, but made no answer.

"And when is my niece expected to depart?" Eirian continued.

"Immediately," said Rother flatly.

"As soon as may be possible," Isolde said quickly, giving him a warning look. "Of course, we will assist with any necessary preparations. But we were hoping to leave tomorrow. Early tomorrow."

Tomorrow! I bit my lip. What about Gabriel? Curse these people! Why *now*, after all these months, must they come back and drag me away? It was ludicrous! I looked hopefully at my aunt. She seemed to have taken an instant dislike to Isolde and Rother. Perhaps – oh, please! – she would stop them.

"Very well," she said, crushing my hopes. "But this is a great inconvenience, and I am seriously displeased. Anne!" Her sudden bellow made the pair jump.

Anne instantly appeared in the doorway; she must have followed my hasty flight earlier. "Yes, ma'am?"

"Since we have less than a full day in which to complete preparations for my niece's journey – preparations which would normally be expected to take a week – I will require you to begin immediately. Fetch Hodge, as you will need him to bring down the large red trunk and the hope chest from the attic."

My temper boiled up at the way I was being ignored. I wanted to leap up and shout: "No one asked me!" But why would they? Nobody ever did. Now I was going back ... and I would miss Gabriel. It was all too much.

Abruptly I stood and, without looking at any of them, stalked out of the room. Behind me I heard the hurried rustle as Rother and Isolde quickly got up and my aunt's perfectly composed voice: "Naturally Lady Alexandra will need to supervise her packing."

Don't be polite on my account, I fumed silently, my stomach churning with helpless rage. I stormed away from the room, heading upwards -- unconsciously making for my favourite room, the library.

My life was being torn apart once more, just as I had started to find some measure of peace. I had resigned myself to never seeing home again; allowed myself to grow comfortable here, to make a true friend -- and now I would never see him again. He hadn't believed that I would be gone when he came back. He had said he would be happy for me, but I knew that was only because in his heart he thought I would still be here. I could see him so clearly -- picture him arriving on the shore as night fell. He would be patient at first, but after a while he would get up, fidget, pace up and down beside the waves. He would be worried, then angry, thinking I had forgotten him.

How would I feel if I thought he had forgotten me? I stopped on the stairs, squeezing my eyes shut against the pain that seemed to hollow out my chest. My breath shuddered out, half sob, half sigh. I couldn't bear it.

"Lady?" Anne's voice quavered on the word. She stood behind me on the staircase -- once again she had followed in my steps. My eyes widened as a new thought struck me, and I turned to look at the little maid.

"Come up to the library, Anne."

"Lady—" She cast a troubled look backwards, obviously guiltily aware of the tasks she had been ordered to complete. She had probably only come after me to try to persuade me to do what my aunt said.

"Don't worry about that," I said impatiently. "We'll start in a minute. Come on!"

I raced up, with Anne following reluctantly behind me. I entered the quiet of the library – a restful silence that welcomed me, rather than the dead stillness blanketing the rest of the house – and waited only for Anne to step reluctantly across the threshold before I firmly closed the door and leaned against it, cutting off her escape.

"I need you to grant me a favour, Anne. It is very important," I said carefully. "They're taking me away tomorrow, and I don't know if I shall ever come back. But there's someone I'm supposed to meet tomorrow night someone very important to me. There's no way I can see him, I know that, but I must get a message to him, Anne. You're the only one I trust to do it."

Anne flushed a pretty pink at the compliment, but the troubled look didn't leave her face. "But ... *him*? Who? And how?"

I understood her meaning well enough, and rushed to reassure her. "He's a friend. I met him walking on the beach, ages ago; you know I often walk by the sea in the evenings, Anne. He'll be there tomorrow evening, expecting to see me. I only want you to say that I am all right – that I'm going home and he shouldn't worry about me. And ... and tell him that I won't forget him. That's harmless enough, isn't it? Will you do it? Please, Anne."

Her worried look faded a little as she realized she wasn't going to be asked to memorize any impassioned speeches.

"Well ... I will try, Lady."

"Thank you, Anne. He'll be there at sunset."

I didn't want to fluster her further now that I had got my own way, so I turned quickly back and opened the door. "I suppose we had better go and start packing."

She sighed with relief. "Yes, Lady Alexandra."

My heart was lighter as I went down the stairs again and walked along the corridor to my room. At least now Gabriel would know that I was all right – and that I had thought of him before I went.

While Anne went to fetch Hodge the footman, I began taking clothes out of the wardrobe and laying them on the bed. I looked at the finely made gowns of heavy wool and light silk, the velvets and the linens. The seamstress had eventually convinced Eirian to allow me one green gown, so dark it was almost black, but most of them were still dove grey, black and dark blue. I remembered, long ago, telling myself that when I left this place I would leave all the new clothes behind. I snorted quietly. I had no choice but to take them now. Not one of the shabby gowns I had brought with me fitted any more – they barely covered my shins or wrists, and the seams strained at my hips and chest while bagging at the waist.

So much had changed since I came here. My hands left the soft cloth and lifted hesitantly to the coiled weight of my hair, then back out, so that I could look at my freckled, stumpy fingers. Had I changed? Yes – oh, yes, in more ways than the physical. In ways even I did not quite understand. It was too much to hope that the Kingdom and home had not also changed. What would greet me when I returned? My father, the Hall... I frowned, feeling as though I had forgotten something. Something wasn't right ... there was something important...

Blood roared in my ears; my vision crawled with silver things that seemed to nibble at the edges of my eyes, like tiny insects. I swayed and slumped down on the edge of the bed.

Slowly the dizziness faded away, along with the thoughts that had triggered it. I blinked, surprised to find myself sitting on my own clothes. As Anne came back in I got to my feet and shook out the rumbled dress I had crushed, and we worked together in silence to pack everything I would need for the journey.

In the months since I arrived at my aunt's house, the tides of Midland had grown strong. That last night, the ebb and rush of enaid was stronger than ever – strong enough to lull me to sleep even though worry gnawed at my stomach. I was not entirely grateful for the favour. My slumber, while deep, was restless.

I had dreams that were both strange and vivid. I saw the great birds again, silhouetted black against the sun. The beating of their wings seemed to echo that of my heart, stirring something inside me that struggled to wake even as I slept. It was a memory, buried like a shell in the sands. The ever-present movement of the tide swirled and tugged at it until it was partially uncovered, and the beating wings of the birds overhead urged to me to dig ... to look, look, look...

Yet somehow, as often happens in dreams, I could not do what I desperately wanted – I could not see what lay in the sand. It seemed to shimmer with silvery swirls, and my sight would not focus. Eventually the birds flew away, and the dream faded. When Anne came to wake me, just before dawn, my eyes were already open, staring at the ceiling.

As the sun lifted its fiery crest over the horizon, I sat in my room, pushing the last pins into the braided coils of hair at the nape of my neck. All my worldly possessions were neatly folded and packed away. Aunt Eirian, Isolde and Rother waited for me downstairs. In a few minutes I would leave the house, probably never to return.

I looked down at my dark green velvet gown. The rough calluses on my palms caught at the soft material as I lifted the skirts and stood, walking slowly out of the room. Anne followed behind me, holding my soft grey woollen cloak and muff. I seemed to be drifting as I moved along the corridor. From the moment I had awoken that morning, a sense of unreality had enveloped me. It was as if my dreams had knocked my mind out of its proper order. I imagined I could feel everything changing ... the world shifting as I moved through it.

I stopped by the window at the top of the stairs and looked out. The two carriages, each with a matched quartet of horses, stood laden with luggage, waiting for me. I thought the images were warped by the thick, bubbled glass of the window, but as I turned to look away, I realized that it was not the glass warping my vision. There was something wrong with my eyes.

I put out a hand against the window frame to steady myself – then quickly withdrew it as the wood shuddered under my touch, like a restless animal. What was happening? What was wrong? I shook my head, turning to look for Anne. I had to tell her ... I was ill; something was wrong ... I couldn't travel like this...

But you're going home. The thought was so clear, it was as if someone had whispered in my mind. I blinked again, relaxing. Of course. I was going home. Everything would be all right there.

I had to go home...

The strength of that longing swamped me. I *had* to get home. I took a deep breath and turned from the window to walk carefully down the stairs. *Home...*

Silvery things darted across my eyes as my aunt stepped forward to give me a hesitant embrace. The warmth of her hold against my skin made me a little less dizzy; I was able to bid her farewell and return her hand clasp.

Then she released me and I was ushered away. The dizziness came back, bringing the silver swirls at the edges of my sight. Cool air ... the sudden light that made me flinch ... more movement – a firm hand under my elbow, helping me into the carriage ... blessed darkness...

CHAPTER
TEN

I have little memory of what came next. This may be as well. I know my vision was clouded with wavering silver that turned all I looked at into a dim muddle of shapes. The world still churned and twisted around me, probably made worse by the jolting of the carriage.

Things gradually became darker. Finally the lurching movements of the carriage stopped.

I was left there in the back, in the dark and cold. I was uncomfortable, twitching fretfully. The silver fog was surrounding me and pushing out all the air until I could hardly breathe. My own restless fidgeting had exhausted me, and I was so tired. Slowly I slipped into an uneasy sleep.

I opened my eyes to the dawning sun, glowing like a milk opal behind a wash of golden clouds. A tree arched overhead, its branches fluttering with spring foliage;

the light rippled over my face like rain. The familiar twisting boughs and knots of bark reassured me. This was the old oak that presided over the gardens of the Hall. Blinking, I sat up, still looking at the sky. Springy flock moss crushed under my palms, filling the air with an astringent scent.

The luminous early-morning gold of the clouds was unblemished, save for three shapes flying in the distance. As I watched, the creatures grew larger and more distinct. They were swans, their snowy feathers shining in the pure light, great wings beating the air in a strangely familiar rhythm. They came closer, closer, until their enormous bodies shadowed my eyes; they wheeled and soared above me, as silent as clouds themselves save for the slow, deep throb of their wings. I craned my neck to look, laughter rising in my throat at the sheer beauty of them.

Remember.

The voice chimed in my head; a voice I knew. Laughter clogged in my throat.

"Robin?" I whispered, eyes straining to make out the shapes of the birds against the glowing light.

Remember... Remember

"David? Hugh?" I cried, lifting my hands up imploringly to the pale birds. The wind of their movement fanned my hair back from my face. "What's happening? Where are you?"

Danger... Remember, Alexandra... Danger.

"I don't understand! Please!"

Remember.

Images flashed through my head. I saw Zella, smiling triumphantly at the centre of a pulsing silver fog. I saw the Circle of Ancestors at night-time, its crown of stones outlined against the full moon, somehow seeming to beckon me. Then the voices returned. This time they were loud enough to make me wince.

Remember. Escape. Awake!

The light snuffed out like a tallow flame. I opened my eyes to darkness.

The clarity of the dream was gone in an instant. My mind fogged as quickly as my vision. I could feel – very dimly – that my throat was parched and my lips cracked. I was weak and shaky. Something was very, very wrong. I was ill. No – this wasn't illness. This was a Great working, a spell. It was killing me.

Yet I couldn't focus on that knowledge. Terrifyingly quickly the dream, my brothers' voices, began to dim in my mind. Even the physical discomfort of finding myself lying on the floor of the carriage, jammed between the seats, was distant and fading. I struggled to hang on to the memory, to my brothers' voices, but the spells on me had been wrought to repel memories of my brothers. The twisting, silvery fog grew deeper. The gritty carriage floor rippled under my cheek and softened like flesh. I struggled for breath, feeling claws tighten around my chest until I could barely breathe, even as the sensation floated away from me. I could not hold on to the pain. My awareness of my body sank down into the mists.

In desperation I searched for something – anything – to anchor myself to. The Hall; Aunt Eirian; the oak tree; my mother's hair; the dawn sky – images flashed through my mind. But the fog knew them, and stole them away. I was losing everything. I was losing my mind.

I was dying.

Then, as clearly as if I stood before it, I saw an image of the sea. The rolling, ever changing sea, now grey-green, now golden, now blue shot with orange. It was never still; never the same ... even Zella could not know all its faces. I saw the sea ... heard it licking at the shore, the calls of the gulls, tasted the tang of salt in the spray ... and at the water's edge, a tall figure in a black cloak waited. His hair blew wildly about his face, and the sprinkling of freckles on his tanned face stood out in the sun. His silvery eyes – such a warm silver, compared to the dark cold of the fog – smiled into mine.

The fog ate at the edges of the memory, trying to envelop it, absorb it. But Zella knew nothing of Gabriel – no one did. The spell could not take what it did not know.

I clung to the sight of his strong hands, the pattern of sand decorating his boots, the way his eyelashes curled. The more details sprang out at me, the clearer he became – and the more the blurring fog shied away.

The tiny dimple in his cheek, the faint scent of lye soap that came from his clothes. Each new memory drove the fog further back. There was a clear space in my mind now, a shining place where my thoughts could gather. I wound all of myself into Gabriel's image, drew his face, his voice, his smell, his tangled hair and freckled nose, into a sword point of blazing certainty and thrust it forward through the swirling blanket of the spell.

The mist parted like an ancient piece of cloth ripped up for rags. I thrust again – the sound of his laughter, the grip of his hand – and it tore. I slashed and hacked at the disintegrating silver – the warmth of his lips against mine – until, suddenly, it was gone.

My mind expanded into the clear space with a roar, like a fire drenched with oil. Everything rushed back. The grit against my cheek, my hip forced painfully against something sharp, my fingers and toes numb with cold. Eirian's house, Isolde and Rother, the trip back to the Kingdom, Zella. The voices from the dream: danger, danger, danger... For an instant I lay gasping as I realized how close I had come to returning meekly home, into the arms of my enemy. How close I had come to death.

Then I was up. I had my woollen cloak in one hand and the other was on the handle of the carriage door, shoving it open. I tumbled out into the night. Wind tore at my hair and clothes as I stumbled, muscles cramping. Clinging to the open door, I managed to keep to my feet, barely. The wind howled through the clearing, almost knocking me to my knees. I was weak and trembling, faint with hunger and thirst. I wouldn't be able to get far like this.

I didn't know where I was, but I did know that I had to get away and put as much distance between myself and these people – Zella's people – as I could before they realised I was gone. Once I was away, there would be time enough to plan. Unfortunately I was not in any condition to flee into the night. My hands shook and I hardly had the strength to stand.

Through watering eyes I saw that the two carriages were stopped in the shelter of a small coppice. The only light was from the gibbous moon tangled in the tossing branches of the trees. Well-wrapped humps near by were the coachmen and grooms. Isolde and Rother must be in the other carriage. Tethered alongside were the eight horses, slumbering happily.

"Perfect," I croaked softly, as a plan formed in my mind. My throat protested painfully at the activity, and I swallowed a cough.

Slowly – for I not only desired stealth but also knew that any quick movement would send me toppling – I shut the carriage door and moved to the back of the second carriage, where my enemies slept, and where the provisions had been stored. With stiff fingers I clasped the cloak at my neck and went to work on the leather straps of the carriage hold. I fumbled and struggled, not even daring to swear under my breath. Finally the straps gave way, and I opened the hold to find a large packing basket on top. I quickly checked the contents: packages wrapped in oil paper and linen and some padded jars.

With some more rooting about I found two leather sacks that were filled with extra bedding. As my cloak snapped and billowed behind me, I pulled most of the blankets out to make room and then packed the food bundles from the basket into them, leaving two spare blankets inside to pad the jars and to provide warmth if I needed it later.

With trembling hands I eased the lid down; but before I could refasten the straps the gale slid in and ripped them from my grasp.

The wooden lid flew up and smashed hard into the back of the carriage, making a hollow boom that could be heard even over the scream of the wind. Terrified, I grabbed for it, but it flapped up and hit the carriage once more before I could shove it down and secure it. The instant it was buckled I flung myself and my bundles down into the undergrowth next to the carriage, out of sight of the door, ignoring the painful bite of a thorny branch against my arm. I made myself as small and still as I could, and held my breath.

There was a slight movement from the carriage, the frame shifting on its wheels as the inhabitants stirred. Then, with a sinking heart, I made out the echo of the door banging back on its hinges. Someone was coming out.

Go back in! Go away! Go away! I bit my lip hard enough to taste blood. The wind dropped for a moment and I heard a snatch of conversation.

"...back to sleep." Isolde's voice, husky and low.

"I heard something, I tell you." Rother, sounding both nervous and annoyed.

"Then at least close the door—"

The wind rose again and whipped the rest of the words away.

I strained my ears against the rush and wail of the weather, tension turning my muscles to stone as I waited for the shout of horror that would tell me they had checked my carriage and found it empty – the raised voices that would rouse the coachmen and grooms to search for me. They couldn't miss me here, and I couldn't possibly run fast enough to escape them. If they checked the carriage, I was done for.

Oh, please, please, *please*...

A long while later I heard the faint thud of Isolde and Rother's door closing, and saw the carriage resettle. My breath escaped in a rasp of relief. Then it occurred to me that Rother might still be outside, and I stiffened again, waiting in dread for him to appear round the side of the carriage. Several more horrible minutes passed, but Rother did not come. Finally I realized that he must have obeyed Isolde, and gone back to sleep without checking. I slumped to the ground, almost boneless with the release of tension, thanking the Ancestors for the inhospitable chill of the night, and the laziness of Zella's servants.

After a few seconds I picked myself up and, after extricating myself with some difficulty from the thorny bush, crept back round the carriage, skirting the sleeping servants widely on my way to the tethered horses. As I approached, one of the horses opened a mild brown eye and whickered quietly. The others came awake and began to shift; one stamped a hoof experimentally.

"Now, now," I whispered, laying my free hand on the nearest mount's warm hide. It calmed immediately at my touch as I sent it messages of reassurance and quiet. Horses are natural herd creatures; such animals, when together, almost share a consciousness. It was easy to reach them all, convey my status as a friend – a dominant one – who needed help to get away. Of course, human words cannot really express such communication, but the horses understood me and acceded to my wish cheerfully enough. They stood, unresisting, as I untied them and then, with an effort that was almost beyond me, managed to seize a handful of mane and heave myself up onto the nearest one's back.

Bit and bridle would have made a worrying amount of noise, but I couldn't help missing them all the same. I'd never been more than passable at riding bareback, and the need to hold the bulging leather sacks securely between my knees and elbows while clutching the mane made it more awkward still. I clamped my knees to the horse's flanks and leaned over its neck as much as I could. Luckily she was a placid mare, and did nothing more than flick an ear at my clumsiness.

Let's go now, I thought to the horse. *Slowly, please, as quiet as possible.*

The horse moved into a slow walk, turning away from the trees. Behind me the other horses were scattering, some moving through the coppice and others heading in the opposite direction to me. They would make it as difficult as possible for the coachmen to catch them. *Thank you!* I called to them. My horse avoided the carriages carefully as I tucked my cloak around my thighs to keep it from flapping behind me.

As we rounded the edge of the coppice, fields opened; to my left the dark blot of a forest climbed a hill and continued along a high ridge. I nudged the mare towards it with my knees. The woods would conceal any tracks and hide me in the daylight if Zella's people tried to look for me on foot. I could also forage for food and find shelter.

I suppose, considering everything, my escape from Rother and Isolde was surprisingly easy. To make up for it, the rest of that night was, well, nightmarish. The wind continued to rise, until it dinned at my ears and almost pushed me from the mare's back. Even after we entered the shelter of the woods, things did not improve. Branches lashed at me and made the horse, sensible as she was, shy and even attempt to rear now and again. I sent all the soothing thoughts to her that I dared, but it was difficult to reassure her when I could hardly think straight myself. The enchanted sleep I had enjoyed seemed to have sapped more energy than if I had spent the week ploughing fields, and my burst of terror-induced energy soon drained away in the unrelenting discomfort and chill of the night. We never moved above a walk as we went through the trees, but since we kept to a steady pace and never stopped, we made good progress. I took some distant pleasure in that, though after a while it all began to blur together into one long, aching torment.

My thighs began to rub and blister with saddle sores. My face grew sticky and disgusting with blood from cuts inflicted by the sloughing branches and blown dirt, and my lips cracked open and bled too. I still did not dare stop. I couldn't risk losing the advantage of my head start; and I also had the worrying suspicion that if I got off the horse, I would not be able to get back on. I hung on grimly to her neck, my body shuddering with a horrible combination of cold and fear and fatigue. My hands grew numb in their death grip on the mare's mane; even if I had wanted to let go and wrestle open a bag for food or water, I didn't think I could move my fingers. The wind gradually died down, but by then I was so tired I hardly noticed.

When the first sickly colour of dawn began to penetrate the shadows of the trees, I stirred weakly on the mare's back and attempted to sit up. A mistake. We were going under a low branch at the time and it hit me smack on the shoulder, knocking me neatly off the horse. I landed in a muddy hollow full of leaf mould and rotting vegetation, the breath forced from my lungs with the impact. At another time such a fall might have done me serious damage, but by then I was so limp with exhaustion that I merely gained some more bruises. I lay there on my back for a long time, staring dazedly up at the black tracery of leaf and bough silhouetted against the sky. Then the mare, having belatedly discovered I wasn't with her, came back to see what I was doing. She lowered her homely muzzle over me – she was a dapple grey, I could now see – and snorted enquiringly, dripping horse slobber on my chest until I lifted my hand and feebly pushed her nose away.

It took a terrifying amount of energy to force myself into an upright position. I sat there, panting in the mud, while I tried to will myself awake. My head was so light that I was afraid it might actually drift up off my shoulders. After a minute I planted a hand on the crumbly forest floor and sent out a weak tendril of awareness through my skin to gather some strength from the land. It was very difficult, and not just because I'd been knocked silly. The enaid was so thin here that I could barely feel it wash around my fingers. I was still in Midland, I realized. Somehow I had expected it to be the Kingdom, though I did not know how long I had been a prisoner. But it was strange; I thought Midland's strength had been growing stronger while I was with Eirian. Apparently that recovery hadn't yet reached this place.

Still, the land shared with me what it had. My back straightened as a little spurt of energy travelled up my fingers into my bloodstream.

The new strength gave me enough clarity of mind to realize that I could not keep going like this. Maintaining my head start would be no good if I perished from starvation, thirst or sheer exhaustion before Zella's people even found me. Besides, I had no idea if I was travelling in the right direction – I might be heading further into Midland with each step, and away from the Circle of Ancestors, my destination. My vision had saved me. Now I must follow its directions.

With the mare – I really had to think of a name for her – contentedly stripping new leaves off nearby plants, I grubbed around until I found the leather sacks, which had fallen with me.

I opened one, and reached in to pull out a random package. Unwrapping it, I found a wedge of crumbly white cheese. Another rummage produced hard biscuits, and a jar of the shredded pickled vegetables that my aunt's cook had made in bulk. The smell of these items made me so hungry that I almost retched. I had no knife. Hurriedly I pulled out one of the spare blankets and spread it on my lap – my skirt was too dirty to consider letting food touch it – then crumbled the cheese onto it. I spread the pickled vegetables onto the hard biscuits with my fingers and crunched them down, glad for strong teeth. Thankfully there was a flagon of wine in the first pack too, which I gulped gratefully. It had been watered, so I didn't worry too much about drinking half of it in one go. I felt I could have gobbled up the contents of both bags, but it was only a few moments before my shrunken stomach protested. I nearly started retching again when I tried to force down more.

Still, the food and drink gave me a little precious energy. After a few more minutes of sitting peacefully, I felt so much better that I became aware of the filth that coated my face. The blood and dirt had now clotted horribly. I was pretty grubby all over. I didn't know how long I had lain in the grip of Zella's working, but I felt as if I hadn't bathed in a week. A new thought occurred to me, and I cringed when I understood that someone must have tended me like child, for there was no urine – or anything worse – on my clothing. Ugh. I hastily shoved that thought away; I simply could not cope with it.

I pulled myself upright using one of the nearby trees and walked around a little. My legs were stiff and sore, and my bottom ached fiercely from the long night's riding, but I ignored the discomfort, because I knew that as soon as I could, I was going to have to get back up on Mare's back and start all over again.

A small way from the hollow where I had fallen, there was a tiny spring, no more than a trickle, bubbling out from a mound of rocks. The water was teeth-clenchingly cold, but I made the best use of it that I could, rinsing my face and hands and the blisters on my inner thighs of blood. I found some splitroot and crushed it, slathering the juice on my cuts and blisters. It would stop them from going bad.

Finally I unbound my disgusting hair and tried to clean it with my fingers and the spring water. When I had finished I wanted to bind it up again – a combination of practicality and habit – but I had lost most of the pins and only the grease and tangles had held it up that long. Wet and fairly clean, I couldn't control the rebellious curls, so I plaited it, tying the end with a ragged bit off the bottom of my petticoat. It was almost long enough to sit on, and made an unpleasant dampness against my back, but there was nothing I could do about it. I looked down at the heavy fabric of my dark green gown. Its once elegant lines were crushed and torn, and it was smeared with drying dirt, streaks of blood and a coat of grey hairs from Mare. My cloak was a little better, but altogether I doubted I made a very respectable picture. Still, my raggedy appearance might prove an advantage if I was careful.

The images from my dream flashed into my mind again. I had to reach the Circle of Ancestors. My dream had left me with a deep sense of urgency that I did not question. To do that, I was going to have to find people, whether within this forest or in the fields beyond, and ask their help. Once inside the Kingdom I was sure I could find my way by navigating the flows of enaid, but here in Midland I was lost. In my new guise as an unremarkable, if grubby, peasant girl, hopefully I could glide beneath the notice of thieves and any agent that Zella might send after me.

I made my way back to Mare, who had settled down for a brief nap, her eyes half shut and one leg slack. She looked quite unkempt herself, dirt- and dust-streaked as she was. I couldn't brush her properly or untangle her mane and tail, but I made an effort to rub her down with the spare blanket I had already ruined, which she thoroughly enjoyed. She was still shabby and begrimed when I finished, but again, this was probably for the best. I slung the now much-misused blanket over her back and led her to a fallen tree which I thought would made a good mounting block.

Here my plan failed. I could not get myself up onto Mare's back. My stiff, bruised legs and hips would not cooperate, no matter how I tried. The patient horse stood placidly enough at first, but after I slithered down her side in the fourth failed attempt, her ears went back and her eyes began to roll expressively. Finally one of the swelling blisters on my thigh burst, splattering gore over Mare's withers and down my leg. Cursing, I admitted defeat, climbing painfully down from the tree trunk and sitting on it. Mare's ears came forward again and she started cropping happily on some wild grass.

Breathing heavily, I was more tired from my brief exertion than I dared own. It seemed I was going to have to walk. Wonderful. I hauled the leather bags into my lap and used the ties at the top to knot them together so that I could carry them across my shoulders. When I had arranged them as comfortably as I could – which was not very – I looked back up at what I could see of the sky through the trees. Dawn had barely arrived. Isolde and Rother might not wake for hours – or they might already be searching for me. Time to move on.

I stood up and laid a hand against Mare's neck, giving in to the temptation to lean on her for a minute, while she snuffled interestedly at my hair. Then I began walking and she followed.

I was grateful for her solid bulk that day. We walked at a steady pace, stopping only once or twice for my essential calls of nature and to eat a little. In all that time I saw no paths or trails made by men, no break in the thick forest cover. But it was not that which disturbed me. Where was the singing of birds? Where was the rustling of foliage, and small animals burrowing and calling out to each other? At this time of year the woods should have been swarming with life, but I hardly saw a single creature. The quiet pressed on me. I, who had been at home in wild places all my life, began to feel the trees closing in, curving above me and pushing down like the narrow confines of a cave.

I was glad when night fell. The gathering darkness hid the crush of trees, and the natural quiet of night-time masked the strange stillness. I risked a small fire – which was difficult enough to light with the lack of enaid – and ate some more of the contents of the sacks. Then I curled up in my blanket and cloak and fell into uneasy sleep. I had hoped for more dreams of the swans, of my brothers' voices, perhaps some sign to tell me that I was travelling in the right direction; but my slumber was untroubled by anything more than the roots digging into my back through my coverings.

The day dawned grey, and a light drizzle filtered down through the trees. I was grateful for the slight shushing noise of the rain, even as I damned the heavy skirts soaking through and the mud that squelched up around my feet. I was weary and aching beyond belief, and my travel became a slow and disheartening trudge. Was I ever going to leave this nightmare? Or was this another spell of Zella's, a trapping enchantment that would befuddle me and keep me wandering for ever? I froze at the idea, causing Mare to whuffle softly in question. The horsey breath on the back of my neck calmed me. No. I doubted Zella was capable of creating so friendly and valuable a companion for me as Mare. This was real life – in all its glory.

When, at midday, I stumbled out of the woods, I was so inured to the misery of the unending forest that I simply carried on walking for several minutes before the different light and the ease of walking broke into my trance of weariness. I blinked, shook my head and pushed back my hood to look around. I stood at the end of a neatly ploughed field, its boundary marked with a tall hedgerow. Below me, more fields stretched away in a series of gently rolling hills.

The fields lacked the bronzy-green glow of health that I knew from the Kingdom's farms; there was mostly greyish mud, and little sign of new shoots. More worrying, the same odd quiet hung over these fields as in the woods. There didn't seem to be any people about: no distant figures working the crops, planting or ploughing; no children running madly around the fields as I had once done. Where had all the people gone?

Turning to look up the hill, I saw a curl of smoke rising behind the wildly overgrown hedge near by, and the peak of a thatched roof. Reaching out, I could feel the presence of animals, bored and not very well fed, and – at last! – people, two of them. I offered a brief prayer to the Ancestors that the farmers would be friendly, and walked on, Mare following faithfully behind me.

I rounded the hedge and stopped dead in shock. I stared, Mare nosing at my shoulder curiously.

I saw not the square, stone Midland dwelling that I had been expecting, but a Kingdom-style wood-frame house, curved in the shape of the long oak boughs used to build it, walls of wattle and limewash, and thatching that ended only a few feet from the ground. To one side a pair of bored cows shared a small byre, and chickens clucked on the gravelled area before it. It looked incredibly homely and inviting to my eyes; but who would have built such a house *here*?

Before I could even begin to answer my own question, a young boy rounded the corner of the byre, a wooden bucket in his arms. He was large for his age, which I thought was about eight or nine, but skinny. He had a round face and straw-coloured hair that poked up in all directions as if he had run his fingers through it.

He froze when he saw me, his arms going limp and allowing grain to spill out from the bucket onto the gravel. The chickens converged on him in a squawking crowd, but his muddy-brown eyes never left my face. I was a little surprised by his look of stunned bewilderment, but supposed he might be frightened at the unexpected arrival of a stranger. I tried a tentative smile to see if it would reassure him. If anything his eyes grew rounder.

"Hello," I said.

He gulped and carried on staring.

"It's all right. I got lost in the woods, and I wondered if you could tell me where I am," I said quietly, using the calm tone I adopted with frightened animals.

He blinked and stared some more. Did I look that awful? I raised a hand self-consciously to my hair, which was escaping from its braid as fast as it could and clustering around my face in twiddly red curls, and tucked as much of it behind my ears as would fit.

"Is something wrong?" I asked finally. "Should I go away again?"

The boy shook his head frantically, almost dropping the bucket entirely as he started into action. "No, no, Lady! Just ... you just wait here, Lady. I'll get my ma!"

He ran to the house, scattering grain left and right, and disappeared through the open doorway. I heard the sound of a woman's voice raised – likely telling the boy off for getting mud and grain all over her floor – and then there was quiet.

A moment later, a short, middle-aged woman with untidy straw-coloured hair appeared in the doorway, wiping her hands on her apron. The boy was behind her, whispering frantically and pointing as he came into view. The expression on her face – one of mixed curiosity and impatience – transformed when she saw me into shock and ... oh, dear, was that *awe*?

"Lady..." she whispered, almost to herself, her eyes as wide as her son's had been. "Oh, Lady. How did you come to be here?"

CHAPTER
ELEVEN

I stood completely still, struggling with myself. The look on the woman's face, the tone of her voice ... all made me want to turn and run from the little house as fast as I could. But I needed their help, and I did not know when I might be lucky enough to encounter people again. And I was so tired.

While I hesitated, she came cautiously towards me and executed a deep, slightly clumsy curtsy. "Lady, would you come inside?" Her voice trembled with anxiety, and she tore her eyes from me to look upwards, as if expecting to see something in the sky.

"I ... why do you call me Lady? You don't know me," I said, eyeing her nervously.

"All of the Kingdom knows you. Please, come inside. It ... it may not be *safe*." She glanced up at the sky again.

All of the Kingdom ... not safe? What? I took a step back.

The woman lifted her hands pleadingly. "My son can care for your horse. Will, take the lady's horse into the shed, and give it a good rub down and some grain."

The boy scurried up to Mare's side, his eyes still as round as hens' eggs. "I'll take good care of the fine beast," he whispered in reassurance, laying a hand on Mare's side. She looked down at him with interest, and before I could stir myself to do anything she was following obediently as he grasped a handful of her mane to led her towards the byre.

Unnerved, I had no choice but to step into the house. Inside, it was dim and warm. Bunches of dried herbs hung from the beams in the ceiling, and pots and treasures decorated the narrow shelf running along the top of the walls under the thatching. There wasn't much furniture, except a large scrubbed table and four rough chairs. Another chair, finer and made for rocking, stood near the fireplace with a hooked rug at its feet, and a fire snickered quietly to itself in the hearth under a stone mantel. The faint smell of beeswax, herbs and baking bread filled my lungs. The smell, so familiar and yet completely forgotten in my time away, brought tears to my eyes, and I blinked furiously. Without even thinking, I had moved forward to stand in the centre of the room. The sound of the door closing and being latched made me spin round.

The woman turned from the door and gave me an apologetic look. "Must be careful." She looked around her, then went to the rocking chair and pulled it back invitingly. "I'm sorry we haven't much, but you can warm yourself by the fire."

Her anxiousness brought a reluctant smile to my lips. "It's the most wonderful thing I've ever seen," I said quietly. "I've been away so long."

The woman bit her lip, and I realized that tears were sparkling in her eyes. "Oh, Lady," she whispered softly. "Poor thing... Please sit down. You must be so weary."

I ducked my head in gratitude and accepted her offer of the chair, relaxing into the curved seat with a sigh as my bruised back and backside almost sang in relief. Most of the tension had gone from me now; I could see she meant me no harm. Yet I was still bewildered by her manner. Who did she think I was?

There was a quiet tap at the door – Will, returning from tending to Mare. The woman went to let him in, and latched the door behind him again. Then she turned to look at me. "I'm Olwyn, Lady, and this is my boy, William."

"I'm glad to meet you," I said, nodding at them, since they seemed to expect it. "Er ... who do you think I am?"

The boy looked at me gravely. "You're the lost lady – the queen's daughter."

I sucked in a sharp breath, staring at him. "What – how—?"

A sudden wave of dizziness made my head spin and I

closed my eyes. I heard a flurry of movement and suddenly a firm hand was pushing me back and holding a cup to my lips. I opened my mouth automatically and gulped down the hot liquid, milk, honey and nutmeg.

"There there, now," came the woman's voice, suddenly soothing and firm as only a mother's can be. "You're naught but skin and bone, and weary as an autumn leaf. Just you rest there."

I breathed deeply, dizziness fading, and opened my eyes to look up at her. She smiled and turned away to put the cup down, but I caught her wrist.

"I thought ... I was still in Midland. This is the Kingdom, isn't it?"

Olwyn nodded and patted my hand gently, before slipping out of my hold. She put the cup on the table.

"What happened?" I asked her helplessly. "What happened here?"

She sighed as she turned back. "A lot, My Lady. Much of it bad." I opened my mouth to ask more questions, but she stopped me with a shake of her head. "I shall tell you anything you ask, Lady, later. After you've rested and eaten properly. It'd be a shame on my household if I didn't look after you right, now wouldn't it? So you rest there, and I'll see what I can do."

I closed my eyes as she bustled away into the room behind me. I was so tired, and suddenly content just to sit there in the warm and do nothing.

I heard the rustle of Olwyn's skirts as she came back

again a few minutes later, and opened my eyes to see her placing a heavy cauldron on the table, followed by fresh bread and a dish of butter. Will sat on the rug by my feet, warming his hands at the fire.

I watched drowsily as Olwyn ladled a steaming substance from the cauldron into bowls and placed one of them on a wooden tray obviously intended for me. I roused myself to say, "I don't eat the flesh of animals."

"This is a nice vegetable broth."

She brought the tray to me, loaded with a full bowl and several slab-like slices of bread, thickly buttered. The delicious savoury aroma wafted up to my nose and sent a demanding growl echoing from my stomach. It was all I could do not to seize the tray from her hands. Instead I waited for her to place it on my lap before falling on it ravenously, scooping up the thick, pale green broth – redolent with the flavours of potato and lovage – with the butter-dripping bread.

Will left the fire and sat down at the table with Olwyn to eat his noonday meal, though rather less hurriedly than me. I finished minutes ahead of them and Olwyn looked up to ask if I would have more. I thanked her, but shook my head. I would let them finish their meal before I tried to question them again. I put the tray down on the floor near my feet and leaned back in the chair, allowing the weight of my body to send it into a gentle rocking motion. The light of the fire played on my eyelids as they fell closed...

* * *

When I woke it was night-time. The fire had died to a banked glow, and a worn quilt was tucked carefully around me. The room was dim; a single taper set on the table provided a soft, gold-edged illumination. Olwyn sat there in one of the chairs, hands busy with needle and thread. I watched her calm, occupied face, letting the peaceful normality of the scene soothe me. Then my throat tickled and I coughed. Olwyn looked up, her serene expression fading to the more familiar one of deference and faint anxiety. I was sorry to see that calm go. As long as I stayed here and disturbed the smooth flow of Olwyn's household, her face would wear those worried lines.

"I'm sorry I disturbed you," I croaked, coughing again.

"No, no. Let me fetch you a drink, Lady. Your voice sounds that sore." She disappeared into the other room and came back with another cup of the honey and milk drink. It was cool this time, probably from the pantry.

I accepted it gratefully, relishing the coolness it brought to my throat and then my stomach as it slid down. "Thank you," I said as I finished it. I stared at the thin sheen left in the bottom of the cup, and wondered how much precious milk the small family would have left after my guzzling. "You've been so good, Olwyn. I don't know how I can repay your kindness."

She looked at me gravely. "It's not kindness, Lady. It's my duty to care for you, as anyone would agree."

I sighed. "Perhaps it's time for you to answer my question, Olwyn, about what has happened while I have been away."

"Mayhap it is," she said resignedly, settling herself into the chair nearest the table and folding up her work neatly on her lap.

"Well." Her deft fingers picked up the needle again as she began her story. "I only knows how to begin at the beginning, so please abide with me, Lady. I suppose it all begins with the land. It's not many a country is as lucky as we've always been here. There's none that don't know the reason why, Lady. Even them like me that never saw the queen – we knew it was her as brought us the blessing of the Ancestors. We knew it was her as kept the Old Ways alive, and we gave thanks for it every day. I told my little ones about her when they were in their cradles. I sung them the songs about how she was the wisest woman in the land and the most beautiful. 'Hair like molten copper and eyes the colour of new leaves, as slender and graceful as a willow branch.'

"And of course we knew about her three fine sons: the oldest to be the king, the next a great commander, and the youngest a famous scholar. And her little daughter, as took after the lady in all things and would follow after her in the Old Ways.

"So, when the queen died ... oh, that was a black day for the Kingdom. And not a sennight had passed before the tales were flying everywhere about *how* she'd died.

About this fearsome creature – nobody knew what – that'd savaged her and about how the king was half mad with grief and went out hunting the thing day after day, and came back each night empty-handed. And then one day he comes back, not empty-handed, but with this lovely young lass he's found in the woods. In the woods like a wild creature, and the stories saying that she was so fair that looking upon her made a man go wrong in the head, and that the young lords were up in arms. And *then* they're gone, banished it's said, by the king himself. And before we can begin to think about that, we hear that the little lady is gone too; spirited away the day before this new girl marries our king and no one knows where or how. Sent away to some far-off place, where she won't be in the way.

"It would make a fine tale for minstrels to sing, Lady. But in real life? What could we think? That our ruler's gone mad? That some fearsome enchantress had cast a spell to kill the queen and take her place? If all this was true, what could common folk do about it? Nothing; that was what my man – my Emrys – said. We must wait for this storm to pass us by, for the young lords to come back, for the king to find his senses.

"Then strange things started happening. Snow falling in the height of summer, falling from a cloudless sky. Weeks of rain, non-stop, in the dry season. Seeds not sprouting; thorn bushes coming up where a farmer had planted nothing but good corn – and overnight too! The birds stopped singing. The green things started to turn grey. The rivers grew muddy and still. Well ... and then the final blow. The king was taking the household away from the Hall. Too old-fashioned, too small. Not grand enough. They were to build a new palace of marble and gold, a place fit for the court – fit for his new wife's beauty. And all able-bodied men were to go at once to help in the building. With the crops failing in the fields and children starving, he's taking away our husbands and sons! He sent purses of gold and told us to buy food from the Midland merchants. And when the men didn't go, he sent soldiers, bought ones, to round them up. My Emrys and my two older boys went five months ago, and I've not heard a single word from them since." She stabbed her needle viciously into the cloth.

"So, us women, we started to think. My daughter and her ma-in-law, and her sisters and their daughters ... we gathered together and we talked. At first we said how, one day, the heir must come back. He and his brothers can't stay banished for ever – not when their people are in need. But how will they know to come back? Why leave at all, if they intended to return? Perhaps they don't. Ah, but what about the lost lady? She was like her mother – taught in the Old Ways. This enchantress couldn't hurt *her* with magic. So even if the heir and the young lords are gone and the king's lost his mind – the lost lady will find her way home, won't she? She'll wait and watch, and one day she'll come back."

Olwyn stopped to study her sewing, and then set it aside to look at me. "Oh, you're not how I expected. You're battered and begrimed and so weary the firelight shines through you – but you've got the wisdom. I can feel it from across the room." She lifted her head, and the flickering light of the taper seemed to fill her eyes with fire. "It's in the blood. You're her daughter. You came back just like we said you would. And now you can save us."

I sat rigid in the chair, numb as I struggled with the implications of Olwyn's story . Father, it seemed, was now completely Zella's creature, sacrificing the good of his people for her whims. My brothers were gone from the Kingdom. And the land … this sad, tired land was the result. Hundreds of years of the Ancestors' wisdom and my mother's golden reign ruined in just one year by a foolish old man. And his ineffectual daughter, I reflected bitterly. Don't forget that.

Perhaps the strange phenomena Olwyn had described were the land's way of fighting against Zella's invading evil. Or perhaps they were only a side effect. Whichever, it was clear that she was sucking the life from the Kingdom. Most disturbing of all were the women of the Kingdom, those misguided, dutiful creatures waiting faithfully for their lost lady to return and save them. They believed in this mythical lady. She would free their menfolk and their king from danger and return the land to prosperity single-handed. The weight of their expectation made me want to shrivel into smoke and drift away into the night. Olwyn wanted me to rescue everyone – me, who couldn't even save herself.

I remembered wryly my childhood dreams, and how I had comforted myself when my brothers' brilliance and my father's indifference had made me feel small. *I would only be Alexandra, and I would be free.* I felt smaller than ever now. Time to face the truth. Zella had thought so little of any danger I might pose that she hadn't even bothered to kill me; instead she had sent me away like a naughty child. I wondered why she had bothered to call me back. Perhaps to play with, for her own amusement. Who could fathom such a mind as hers?

In any kind of combat with Zella I did not stand a chance. She was cunning and ruthless, a shape-shifter and an enchantress. She had bested my mother, and Branwen had been a wise woman rejoicing in the full bloom of power. I could never defeat Zella alone. Neither could I admit defeat without trying. I sighed deeply as I made the admission to myself. Not while my home and my people needed me so desperately. Not while my brothers wandered in exile somewhere. Not while Zella walked freely in the world enjoying the warmth of the sun and the sweetness of the air, and my mother's ashes shifted restlessly on the wind. It wasn't too late. The people still remembered the Old Ways. There was still life in the land. It could recover. The people could recover. But before there was any chance of that, Zella had to be defeated.

The first step I must take was to seek out the Circle of Ancestors. Even if my dream was not true, the Circle was a refuge for followers of the Old Ways. I could wake the stones again to speak to the wise women – to Angharad. It would not be easy because I wouldn't be able to navigate the currents of enaid to find it, and I had no idea where its true location was. Perhaps...

"Olwyn. I do not know if I can do what you want," I said quietly, meeting her eyes. "But if I am to try, then I need your help."

"I'll help however I can," she said matter-of-factly.

"Then think on this. I need to find a sacred place: we call it the Circle of Ancestors. I do not know where it may lie – I have never travelled to it on foot – but it is a hill, shaped like an upturned bowl with a smooth top and crowned by a circle of tall stones. Do you know of any such place?"

Olwyn tilted her head, thinking. "I have heard of a place like that, though it might not be the one you describe. It is a strange-looking hill, flat on top, where no one ever dares go, though I couldn't say why. They call it Olday Hill. But I never heard tell of any stones on the top. That doesn't mean they aren't there, of course."

I bit my lip. Surely the stones would be remarkable enough to be talked about, if Olday Hill was the Circle. The name, though, seemed to suggest it had something to do with the Old Ways. "Can you tell me any more about it?"

"Not much, Lady. I've never been there myself, you see. There's a story that a dragon sleeps coiled around the base of the hill, – and he'll wake if the Kingdom's ever in peril." Her lips quirked. "If that's so, he's a heavy sleeper."

I blinked. "A dragon?" My mind worked quickly. The massive ripples in the land that the Ancestors had built with their earthworks: people who knew no better might easily make up a tale to explain them. What more natural than that the story should call the dragon a guardian – for that, in fact, had been the purpose of the building of the Circle. It *had* to be the place.

"Is it far from here?" I asked.

"Less than half a day's ride, Lady. Will could lead you there if you wanted; he went that way with his father last year." She smiled a little sadly, I thought, at the mention of her absent husband. Would Will ever see his father again? He would if I had anything to do with it.

I nodded decisively. "Then we will go tomorrow, if you can spare him." I looked at her expectant face and tried a smile. "I'll do my best, Olwyn. That I *can* promise."

Whether it would be enough was another matter.

She sighed and closed her eyes, whether in relief or disappointment I couldn't tell. Then she picked up her sewing again, and settled back.

"You'll need a good night's rest then, Lady. You go back to sleep; I'll watch over you."

I didn't bother to argue that I needed no one to watch over me. She would just tell me it was her duty – and besides, it was comforting to have her there. No one had watched over my sleep for a very long time.

For Olwyn's sake I rested my head against the back of the chair and turned my face away so that she wouldn't see the telltale gleam of the light in my sleepless eyes.

CHAPTER
TWELVE

Mists curled up damply from the fields as Will led me to Olday Hill on Mare's back. The sun had been muffled in cloud from the moment it lifted, and the chill was deep. I huddled deeper into my heavy cloak and looked down at Will's damp hair. He was well wrapped too, but I worried that the long walk might tell on him. I'd offered several times to dismount and let him ride Mare for a while, but he'd refused with every appearance of repugnance, marching happily on. In truth, even after walking half the morning he seemed haler than I did sitting on the horse. A night's rest in a warm house and good food had done much to strengthen my body, but the dreary greyness of the day and the fearful anticipation of what might come contrived to sap the energy from me. The Kingdom shouldn't be like this. I could feel the tiredness of the land in every waft of fog, like the sweet, weary breath of a dying man.

Gradually the lay of the fields under Mare's hooves changed; we were walking through a series of slowly rising inclines and shallow dips, each one growing more pronounced. The rise and fall of the land was too regular to be natural. These must be the earthworks I had seen from the Circle; we *were* in the right place.

After a few minutes more I began to feel, on the edge of my perception, a gentle hum, like the sound of bees on a lazy summer afternoon. Inexplicably, my mood began to lift and my breath quickened in my throat. The weak eddies of enaid in the wind and soil that had so depressed me were gaining strength. Soon they had grown into the plentiful rush that I had been used to in the Kingdom. I hadn't realized how much I had missed the warm buffeting sensation on my skin. I had not felt it since I left my aunt's house, which seemed like aeons ago. A week? Only a little longer than that. I was a creature of the enaid, and without it I diminished quickly.

I basked in the increasing power. In its rush along the channels of earth, it swirled and broke around me and my body sucked in the warmth and energy. A fizz of excitement began in the pit of my stomach; a low, happy laugh escaped my lips. I was home – really home! The strength of the tides was now enough to intoxicate me. We must be very close.

Will had looked up at my laughter. In my sudden elation it took me a minute to realize that, rather than sharing my pleasure, he looked white and frightened. In the same instant, Mare stopped walking and would not budge, no matter how much I urged her.

"What's wrong?" I asked, addressing both beast and boy.

Rushing and pushing ... hurts ... too loud ... were the sensations Mare conveyed to me. Will was even less communicative. He merely grunted and shook his head as if he was in pain.

"Will, what is it?" I demanded, alarmed.

"Don't know. Something ... my ears. Like water. It wants to push me away." He lifted his hands as if to cover his ears, then dropped them again.

I was sharply reminded of my brothers' reactions when Zella had first come to the Hall. All the flow of enaid wanted was to be on its way, and if the path of least resistance was through the fibres and bones of your body, then so be it. Perhaps it could be overwhelming to an untrained person when it was this strong – there had to be a reason why ordinary people never came close enough to see the stones on the hill.

I slung my leg over Mare's back, wincing at the pull on my heavily bandaged, inner thighs, and slid to the ground. Mare's shoulder was rock hard and her dapple-grey hide was dark with sweat despite the cold and the easy pace of the walk. I patted her gently, sending reassurances as I unloaded the saddlebags that Olwyn had slung over her withers. The packs were stuffed with all sorts of useful items that I had accepted gratefully, and they weighed comfortingly against my back as I arranged them over my own shoulders.

"This is as far as you need come with me, Will. I want you to take Mare and go home to your mother."

"Ma said—"

"It's all right," I told him firmly. "I can find my own way from here. Please tell your mother that I'm very grateful for all she's done, and that I will keep my promise. I don't know if I'll see her again. She's not to worry."

"But—"

"Go on. I want you home before nightfall. Take good care of Mare for me – she's a fine horse." I caressed her velvety muzzle a last time, and she managed a gentle nibble of my hair despite her discomfort.

Before he could protest again I turned away, calling on the abundant enaid present to thicken the fog behind me so that I disappeared quickly from view. I waited to hear the quiet thud of Mare's hooves before I began walking again.

Olday Hill loomed before me, as if it had only waited for me to be alone before it showed itself. Against the shifting white of the mists it looked less like a hill and more like a small black mountain that had sprouted from this flat plain. It seemed unnaturally forbidding – so much so that I wondered if the effect was the first of the protective spells embedded in it. But its shadowy hulk could not frighten me. I had come so far to reach this place; all I had to do was penetrate the protective spells Angharad had spoken of and reach the peak.

As I came closer, I saw that the pattern of coiling ditches continued up the hill itself, curling around its conical shape and creating an effect like giant steps. Perhaps I could follow the path of enaid, circling the hill instead of trying to walk vertically. It would take longer than a straight path, but if I stayed within the ditches surely I could not succumb to any misdirection spell.

The enaid pulsing in my blood would allow no apprehension. I placed my foot in one of the ditches on the steep slope and began to climb.

The fog wreathing the hill made it difficult to choose my steps, but as I had hoped, the lay of the ground and the strong push of enaid at my back made it impossible to go astray, even when, about ten minutes later, I encountered the first of the defences. Touching it was a strange sensation. I could not see a thing, but it was solid and faintly warm beneath my hands, and impenetrable.

A childhood memory gleamed in my mind. My mother in a playful mood, rubbing soap in her hands and then circling finger and thumb to blow a fragile, iridescent bubble. It had landed on my skin, trembling for an instant before disappearing with an almost inaudible pop. That was how the barrier felt under my hands. I pushed against it, and slowly it yielded to let me through. Heady with pulsing enaid, it hardly occurred to me to feel surprise at how easily the barrier gave way, though I did wonder if the spells recognized me. I emerged unruffled on the other side and carried on. The further I travelled, the closer together the barriers came; but they did not trouble me.

Then my head broke out of the fog. Brilliant sunshine, the deep, honey gold of late autumn, flowed down to warm my scalp and face, spilling over my shoulders and arms, my hips, and then to my feet as I rose higher. My final step took me over the lip of the hill onto the plateau, between two of the towering stones.

The sky curving above me was so vivid that it hurt to look up, with clouds like wisps of carded wool scattered here and there. Below, it was as if the fog had never been; the land was not soggy brown, but covered with the amber stubble of recently harvested fields and the forests that clad the rising land were a blaze of red and orange. I wondered what time I looked on, even as I devoured the sight.

I thought of Gabriel, and how much he had wanted to see this country; how much I wanted to show it to him like this, in its glory. A great flood of love shook me to my bones as I stared out, the megaliths rising up around me in silent salute. This was the Kingdom as it should be, as Gabriel must see it. I would have it this way again, if I had to die to make it so.

I pulled off the leather sacks and let them fall. In a daze of remembrance my feet took me across to look out at the sea, as they had on my first visit to the Circle. The same sea that Gabriel and I had danced in together. Today it was a sparking silver crest on the horizon, and without even thinking, my hand came to rest on the rough surface of the stone immediately to my right.

Nothing happened. I frowned. I should have known better than to think it would be that easy. Had I wasted my time coming here?

A gentle sigh rose from the stones, as if in response. And then Angharad was there.

She said nothing, just reached up with one weathered hand and cupped my check. Her expression as she studied my face was one of inexpressible sadness; she squeezed her lids shut briefly, then heaved a deep sigh and looked at me again.

"Well," she muttered. "You've grown." She patted my check and then dropped her hand.

I sucked in a shuddering breath and pulled away from her. Her hair, which had been deep glossy red when I saw her that first time, was now streaked with silver, and her face was deeply lined, the skin almost translucent. Her proud bearing could not hide the stoop of age. She had aged thirty years.

"Yes," she said, as if she had heard my shocked thoughts. "This is a different Angharad. And I see before me a new Alexandra."

I nodded, speechless.

A small smile tugged at her lips. "Though in some

ways you are still the same, I see. You're still far too good at listening, and not good enough at talking. I know why you've come ... but I don't think I can help you, my dear."

I frowned, torn between happiness at seeing her again and disappointment at her words. "Do you know everything that's happened?"

"As much as the enaid could whisper to me, yes. I know what evil has overtaken the Kingdom, and what you have suffered by it. And I know the question that you need to ask. So ask it, my dear."

I was puzzled by her manner, but went ahead. "I suppose ... I wanted to ask about my brothers. Where they are. If they're all right."

Angharad sighed. "Oh, child... Can't you see them?"

I stared at her. "What are you talking about? They were banished from the Kingdom. There's no one here but us."

As I spoke I looked around me: the Circle was empty. Then something made me look up. Far above, so far that they were little more than pale specks in the sky, a trio of swans circled and wheeled on the wind. *My dream...*

I blinked, and they were gone. The sky was empty.

Suddenly I saw myself lying on the floor of Zella's chamber, paralysed and blinded – and in my mind the images of my brothers, screaming with agony, their bodies twisted and tormented by that woman's foul spell. But it had been a nightmare. *Only a nightmare...*

"Angharad!" I gasped. "What did Zella do to my brothers? What happened?"

"You know what happened; you saw it yourself," she said gravely. "Now it's up to you to repair the damage."

"But ... but you have to help me!" I stammered. *"Please."*

"No, Alexandra," she said firmly. "You don't need my help." She hesitated. "Your brothers' souls are trapped between this world and the next. You have to free them. Once that is done, everything else – the wicked creature Zella, the Kingdom's dying enaid – will be set right. That is all I can tell you; for this is a tangle beyond anything I've ever known, and you are the only one with the skills to fix it. Any help I might try to give could only harm them – and you – more, believe me."

I felt my knees buckle and fell in a heap at her feet. "I don't ... I can't..." I whispered. My head spun. They're not dead. They can't be dead. They wouldn't leave me...

She crouched to take my hands, squeezing my fingers gently. "Listen to me, Alexandra. Your poor, foolish mother may have kept you from exploring your gift, but it is there, nonetheless. You are a wise woman, and what's more, I think you're one of the most skilled cunning women this land has ever seen. So use your gift, and your knowledge. Trust yourself. You know what to do, if you will trust yourself to do it."

She released me. A moment later, I heard a sigh rise up from the stones, and knew that Angharad was gone.

I sat for a long time in the Circle, struggling to understand what Angharad had said. My brothers were not in exile; they had been with me all along. I had seen the great, pale birds so often in my dreams, and even at other times, yet I had never thought, never realized... Were they aware of who they were? Or who I was? Oh my poor dears – do you suffer?

Eventually I wiped my wet face on my cloak, took a deep breath and forced myself to do what I knew I must. Mentally I reached for my mother's book and began to turn the pages. I remembered spells of healing, of binding, making and unmaking, calling and returning. What charm or enchantment could possibly fit such a situation as this?

After considering and discarding a dozen ideas, I finally remembered a powerful work near the back of the book – one Mother had never had to use. The working's purpose was to capture stray souls and return them to their bodies. The book said that the working was usually required when a person had been ill for so long that they lost the will to survive, and their soul drifted into the ether between this world and the next while their body still lived. It was the only thing I could think of which might reclaim my brothers' souls from where they were lost.

The working required the gathering of the stalks of a blistering nettle, sometimes called wanton's needle. The stalks had to be crushed and dried by hand, and stripped into flax. The flax could then be knotted, woven or knitted into a tunic – three, in this case – for the lost spirit. Once it was complete, a further, master charm would call the spirit to its tunic and bind it into the nettles, and when the tunic was placed on the body of the afflicted person, their soul would return to its proper place. And there was something else. From the moment the first nettle was harvested, the weaver must remain utterly silent. Not a sound, neither of joy nor of pain, must pass their lips, or the spell would be ruined.

If I did have a Great gift it should be within my power to complete the working. There were two problems. The first was that the nettle's sting caused dreadful pain and swelling to the flesh; but that problem I believed I could overcome or endure. The second was more difficult. With my new memories about that awful night in Zella's room, I realized it was possible that my brothers had no bodies to return to. Once I had recalled their spirits, what would I do?

Angharad said that I must set them free in order to make things right. Yet how could I bear to let them go?

I stood, picking up my packs and feeling the weight of me choice settle over my like a heavy mantle. I did not look back at the tall stone – Angharad's stone – that stood proudly on the far side of the Circle, looking out to the sea. Instead I walked forward, through the Circle and onto the narrow outer rim of the plateau. The next step saw my feet disappear into a moist, curling fog; then the darkness of the mists closed over my head like a damp blanket. I stood in the stream of enaid, absorbing the energy, as before; but this time it was different. Something was wrong.

There was a taste in the wind, coppery and thick, that clogged sourly in the back of my throat. Beneath the lazy-bee hum of the Circle's power I could sense something else – the mad drone of swarming wasps. The two kinds of energy mixed oddly, seeming to warp and swirl against each other like the patterns oil makes in water.

I knew the smell; I knew the sound. There was danger here. Something waited for me at the base of the hill.

Zella.

CHAPTER
THIRTEEN

I took shallow, quick gulps of the sour air, my hands clenching into fists. I was not afraid, I realized dimly. I was angry. After everything she had done – everything she had taken from me – she dared intrude, in the sacred place of the Ancestors.

Let her come, I thought grimly.

Stiff with tension, I followed the circuitous path of the energy river to the foot of the hill. This time the defence bubbles let me through with no resistance, perhaps because I was travelling away from the Circle, and my progress was much faster. Even so, by the time the glossy green of the hillside turned to the greyish mud of the field, I was scintillating with a dangerous combination of borrowed strength and anger.

There was a stir in the mists. Tiny whirlwinds rose up

before me, sucking away the cover of the fog until there was a small, smooth aisle of clear space leading from my feet. Into the patch of clarity stepped Zella.

She presented the sort of picture that should instantly have made me feel grubby and unworthy in every way. She was wrapped in a voluminous cape of dull gold lined with luxurious white ermine. Topazes the size of the top joint of my thumb dangled from her ear lobes. Her long honey-coloured hair was dressed coiled smoothly in intricate knots; thick chestnut streaks were visible around her hairline. The sight of that colour sent a razor thrill of hatred shooting up into my brain.

I drew myself up and met the darkness of her gaze with all the force I could muster, feeling a hot flash of triumph when her eyes instinctively flickered away before returning to meet mine. Surprise and annoyance tightened her mouth, and then dropped away into a smile.

"So..." She drew the word out, her rich voice edged with malicious humour. "You've finally crawled back."

"Why didn't you kill me?" I asked abruptly.

She broke into a gurgle of low laughter that grated across my nerves. "Oh, I tried. I would have enjoyed nothing better than to bite out your throat; but despite my charms those bovine household people still retained their affection for you. They insisted on staying with and caring for you and I couldn't risk an open killing so soon. It might have damaged my hold over them. So I poured you full of enough poison to drop a whole village of snivelling humans. *You wouldn't die.* Since I was still drained by our little altercation over your brothers, I only had enough strength for trifling spells, and I was forced to think of another plan to get you out of my way. Your father was most obliging. He never did care for you overly much, did he? By now I imagine he's forgotten you ever existed."

Zella's verbal blows glanced off me; I had faced my own failings and my father's long ago. Unmoved, I studied her carefully. She seemed to be revelling in this opportunity to explain her own cleverness. Perhaps I had a chance... I began to run through spells of deflection and attack in my mind.

"Why did you send for me?" I asked carefully.

Her face hardened. "This land. It will not yield to me. It defies me – *me!* – hoarding its power in places like this." She cast a look of loathing at the hill looming behind me. Did it make her nervous? "Still trying to reward the efforts of the vile farmers, wasting power on filthy fields and base crops!" She stopped abruptly, fingering the jewel in her left ear while the anger on her face transformed with frightening speed into pleasant sweetness. When she spoke again her voice was level.

"As your mother was neatly disposed of, I eventually realized it must be you. Somehow your life was giving the land the will to resist me. I could feel the growing strength in Midland, reaching out to the Kingdom. Did you think I would not notice? You don't even know enough to hide your presence. I decided to bring you back and end your connection with the land. I know the ways. It might not even have killed you – you could have been useful to me, stripped of your will and under my control. Unfortunately those incompetents I sent did not cast my spell net properly, and you escaped. Perhaps you thought yourself clever, but you have gravely miscalculated in returning here. I have gorged on the life of the Kingdom while you were pouring yours into Midland. I am stronger than you now, stronger than anyone you have ever known. It is time to rid myself of you once and for all."

She flung up her hand in a lightning-quick gesture and a burst of sickening red light exploded before my eyes, blinding me momentarily. I felt the death spell she had been constructing while she spoke leave her fingers. It bubbled towards me, growing into a boiling wave of blood red that would drain me and leave me a desiccated husk.

I stood fast, opening my mind, calling on the enaid that coursed through and around me, on the land beneath my feet and the sky above. *I am a wise woman. Answer me ... answer my call...*

Power surged through me, sluicing down my arms like a waterfall as I lifted them. There was a burst of light; my dazzled eyes saw a swan spreading its great, glowing wings through the mist before me; and the two spells collided with a sizzle like burning meat. The light of the swan's shape shone through the blood red, as pure and brilliant as the new moon on the sea. Zella's spell evaporated, curling off in wisps of oily brown smoke. Slowly the glowing light faded away.

Zella's round cheeks had gone pink with rage. "What is this?" she spat. "You're nothing! You can't do that!"

Her hand whipped up, shining with livid red power – but this time I struck first. All my anger and anguish and the dangerous feeling of euphoria engendered by my first victory combined in a bubbling wave of power. I felt it rise up within me like a tide, seething and roaring, almost lifting me from my feet. It burst into the air with a noise like a thunderclap. Before Zella could move it had enveloped her. Thunder sounded again, rumbling and resounding through the mist until it almost deafened me. The light flickered and brightened, and I flung up a hand to protect my eyes. Then, with a sort of sigh, the light dimmed and the spell died into darkness.

Zella was on the ground several feet away, her draperies and fine furs crumpled and singed around her. She lay still, and I felt a terrible thrill of joy – the joy a hunter feels when he sees the blood of his kill.

Then the bundle of material stirred, and she sat up slowly. I saw immediately that I had not managed to do her any real harm. Her expression was not of pain, but of shock and annoyance.

My heart sank, but I spoke calmly, forcing my voice to steadiness. "It seems you're not as clever as you'd like me to think, Stepmama. You've had your time to speak; now you can listen, and I advise you to mark my words. I'm going away now, because I have a task to accomplish, and I don't know how long it might take. But one day, Stepmama, I will return, and when that day comes, all your spells and tricks will count for naught. I will rid this land of you and avenge my family if it takes the last breath of my body. So enjoy your reign here; it will not last for long." I stopped, astonished at my own eloquence.

"*You* threaten *me?*" she growled incredulously, her voice cracking and deepening as she spoke. "Threaten *me? You?*"

The black eyes opened wide, their darkness spilling over onto her face until the delicate features sank back into warped shadows; twisted and re-formed into something ... different. She bared her teeth, gleaming white incisors growing visibly as I watched. The chestnut streaks in her hair began to ripple down, spreading over her lengthening face like veins, carrying bristling, fox-coloured fur with them. Her body bowed and stretched as she dropped onto all fours.

A belated stab of alarm penetrated my anger, and I backed away. She was taking her natural form – the form that had bested Mama – and the change was almost complete. There was no time for further thought.

I turned and ran.

Sucking up power from the land under my feet and the air around me, I flung myself forward. The first step was almost impossible. It was like pushing through another bubble, but this time the bubble pushed back. Rushing air plastered my gown to my body and threatened to rip the hair from my scalp. I concentrated on getting my foot down, ignoring the screaming pain from the bones in my leg as they protested against the strain. My arms, forced behind me by the speed of the movement, felt like they were being ripped from their sockets. I gritted my teeth, clenched my fists, and pressed forward.

I can do this. I am a Wise woman.

My foot hit the ground with a jolt that nearly knocked me over, and I was out of the fog into weak sunshine. I lifted my other foot, risking a brief look over my shoulder. I saw Olday Hill rising up behind me, still wreathed in fog, and a dark blot, low to the ground, moving through the mists towards me with incredible speed. Then I shoved forward again and the hill was torn away. Trees and fields whipped past on either side in a greyish-green blur; before me there was only a narrowing point of light.

Touching the ground once more, I slipped down damp grass on a steep slope, tumbling head over heels to land at the foot of a little hill. The hard objects in the leather packs jabbed painfully into my spine before

I managed to scramble to my feet and push myself on again. The world disappeared into rushing air and lines of undulating colour, the light ahead growing brighter. Then something shifted inside me and I knew I had travelled far enough. I felt a flare of warmth and something like welcome. It was as if an old friend had reached out and taken my hand. This was the right place to stop.

The jolt as I halted was enough to drive the breath from my lungs and send me toppling onto my face. I lay still for a moment, winded, then sat up, shoving the bags of provisions off my shoulders with relief.

I had landed in a large clearing in a forest – a bright, healthy green forest, filled with the cheerful chatter of birds and animals that continued undisturbed by my arrival. Real blue-yellow spring sunlight dappled through the trees and sprinkled over the forest floor like carelessly dropped coins. A few steps away, its slate roof almost hidden under the canopy of a vividly green beech, was a tiny stone cottage. It was tumbledown and obviously abandoned; the door was nothing more than a few splinters held together by the iron hinges from which it hung crookedly, and a climbing hops plant had grown over most of its face and through one of the windows. The outer walls looked solid, though, and it would provide a lot more shelter from wind and rain than the cover of trees alone.

Best of all, sending my mind down into the rich soil, I

could feel a tremendous rush of power. I let it take me, ebbing and washing through the land, up into the trees and plants, adding a gleam of gold and warmth to the air and following the silver paths of rivers and streams.

Suddenly my skin shivered and covered in goose pimples, as if in response to a touch – a loving caress, alien and yet familiar. I caught my breath. *Gabriel.* For a split second I thought I could sense his presence; could almost imagine his warmth against me, smell his hair, hear his breath. Then the feeling of closeness was gone; but the sensation of rightness, of welcome, remained. I sighed. Perhaps it was only my imagination, but I was sure I knew where I was now.

Midland.

I stared around me, my brow wrinkled in thought. What was it that John had said to me when we first came here? That Midland had never recovered after its wars; I had felt the truth of that myself. Now the land seemed to have healed. Gone was the tired wistfulness that had saddened me so. This place sang with happiness and love, of the joy of new things growing and being born. I had felt the tides gaining strength at Aunt Eirian's house but I had not realized the healing had extended so far. What could possibly have brought about such an amazing change so quickly, after so many years of illness?

Zella had said she had felt a growing power here. She thought it was mine. Could it be? Had *I* done this? Was this what Angharad had been trying to tell me in the

Circle? That if I trusted myself, if I managed to ... I swallowed, but forced myself on ... to free my brothers, then I might also have the power to heal the Kingdom?

Surely not even my mother had been able to generate enough strength to replenish a whole land. I shook my head. However Midland had come to be healed, and whether I had anything to do with it or not, I had other things to concentrate on now.

I got to my feet and went to inspect the little cottage. It really was tiny, with no dividing walls inside. The outer walls were well put together and solid. Despite all the mess, the place could not have been deserted for more than a year. On the right there was a small hearth, which was full of soot and debris. I knew the chimney must have a bird's nest in it – and sure enough, when I investigated, a family of starlings had made it their home. Asked nicely, they agreed to leave, if I would remove their nest without ruining it and carry the still flightless chicks to a new home. I couldn't help but laugh at the high-pitched shrieking the babies made and at the little crowns of feathers that stuck up haphazardly from their heads. Gabriel would have loved to see this. I sighed as I tucked the last chick into the nest, now relocated to a tree near the cottage, then I went back to work.

The floor was thick with dirt, leaves and rubbish. The two tiny windows at the front had lost their shutters and the door disintegrated as soon as I touched it. There was a little alcove to one side of the fireplace. It held a tall besom, a wooden bucket with a piece of soap stuck to the bottom like a fossil, and, on a shelf, some folded rags and a rusty cooking pot. I carried all these out and shook the dust and cobwebs off them, then took the bucket and went searching. There must be a well or spring near by, or no one would have been able to live in the cottage. After fighting my way through the overgrown remnants of what had once been a herb and kitchen garden, I found a stone-lined pit with low walls and a peaked wooden cover. The metal crank to bring the water up was so stiff that I almost had to stand on it to get it to move, but the water, when it came up, was sweet and clean. I poured it into my wooden bucket and left it in the sun, hoping that the soap would dissolve. If not, I'd have to go looking for some plants that would lather up. In the meantime I took the besom and attacked the floor and chimney.

By evening I was tired, sweaty, sore and covered in dirt and soot. But the little cottage was sparking clean, the floor scrubbed and scattered with sweet-smelling herbs, the fireplace and chimney in use to burn the rubbish I'd swept out, and a cosy bed of leaves, grasses and moss made for me in one corner.

My stomach's loud growl interrupted my satisfaction. I hadn't eaten since Olwyn's generous breakfast that morning – good Ancestors, had that only been this morning? – and thought of the leather packs I had tucked neatly into one corner of the cottage. The generous woman had stuffed them with what I was sure was every bit of food she could spare, but a great deal of that might now be crushed beyond recognition. I had not been able to protect the packs during my morning's adventures and I'd squashed them while falling more than once. In any case, it would do me no harm to forage for my supper.

I went searching for good things to eat, gathering wild cress and onions, and horse mushrooms from the forest floor, collecting my bounty in my skirt. A little way from my new home there was a tall granite formation, the remains of a long-eroded cliff perhaps. As I looked up at its mossy top, I saw the giant golden stacks of the mushroom called chicken of the wood on account of its meaty rich flavour growing layer upon layer in at least a dozen of the trees around it. Half of one of those mushrooms would feed me for a whole day. Gently I laid the contents of my skirt in a hollow on the ground, then kilted up my dress and petticoats and found a foothold in the pitted surface of the stone pile.

My old skill at climbing came back to me, and I clambered up the side with ease. With a grunt of effort, I pulled myself onto the overgrown top of the formation and looked around. There was a lovely big, golden mushroom just within arm's reach, and after a bit of leaning and near toppling I managed to detach a large chunk of it and tuck it into a fold of my tied-up skirt.

I looked down past the moss-and ivy-covered ledge on which I was perched. The side I had climbed was very nearly vertical, but through the thick cover of leaves and small saplings on the other side I thought I could make out a gentler slope. I manoeuvred myself around and began backing down the incline. Sure enough, the gradient was much gentler. What I hadn't realized was that the carpet of damp moss and loose soil would also make it much more slippery. I had only made it halfway down before my reaching foot slid off an unexpected deposit of wet leaves and I lost my grip on the granite wall. Crashing through self-propagated bushes and saplings, I slithered down, scrabbling vainly for a hold and dislodging loose rocks and vegetation as I went. Eventually my feet hit the bottom and I fell off, landing hard on my backside.

My groping hand had grabbed hold of something as I came down, and the skin of my palm now exploded with searing pinpricks of pain. I instinctively stifled a curse of pain as I nursed my burning hand and looked up.

All around me and halfway up the stone formation they grew: vivid green nettles, their tips decorated with tiny purple flowers and an impressive display of long spiny needles. Dazed, I stared at the plants, thanking the Ancestors I had not cried out when I touched them.

The nettles were wanton's needle. My task, it seemed, had officially begun.

CHAPTER
FOURTEEN

I trudged back to the cottage in the fading light, trying to ignore the incessant, hot throbbing of my hand. I tried to ignore it as I cleaned out the old cooking pan and as I searched for carrots and potatoes in the wild kitchen garden behind the house. I tried to ignore it as I sliced up my vegetables and mushrooms using a sharp knife I had found wrapped up in the bottom of one of the packs and fried them over the fire, and as I ate the delicious savoury mess out of the pan.

By the time I had finished my supper and prepared for bed, my left hand had turned a frightening purple, my finger joints swelling until the knuckles were like smooth, round berries. My palm, which had taken the brunt of the stings, was twice as fat as normal. The places where the stings had gone in were a nasty, oozing purplish-black colour. It felt as though I had thrust my hand into a fire.

What was worse, I could not even cry with the pain as I longed to – no noise, the book had said. So my eyes watered silently as I lay down on the cushiony moss and reeds and awkwardly spread my cloak over myself. The book said it would be terrible, I reminded myself. It said it was almost impossible – and if both my hands swell up like this, then it surely will be. But I have no choice.

My lecturing did no good. The pain was too intense to ignore, and I could not sleep. Near dawn the pain began to subside a little, or perhaps my fatigue numbed it for me, and I fell into a troubled doze. I dreamed uneasy dreams. My brothers flew through a midnight sky, then landed on a white stone tower where they rooted and bloomed, turning into glorious roses. The tower itself begin to branch and twist until it was a white, barren tree glowing with my brothers' vibrant flowers; and their petals fell and became white feathers once more, and the shining feathers washed together and turned into a pale, frothing sea that whispered my name in Gabriel's voice...

I emerged from sleep to find my hand back almost to its normal size and colour, and a pair of skylarks singing good day to me from the windowsill. I looked down at the remaining redness of my hand and wondered, uneasily, if I had helped the healing along in my sleep. The tides here were so strong that even my unhappy dreams could have been enough to call on the enaid.

Surely that was not allowed. I could not have ruined things before they had even begun!

As I sat there dithering, I remembered something. The book had set out clear rules: I must harvest the nettles by hand and knit or weave them into tunics for my brothers, and so long as the task endured I must not utter a sound in either pain or joy. It had said absolutely nothing about workings being forbidden. I could assume that charms should not be used to ease my pain ... but the spell had not said any such thing.

I had a choice. I could follow the rules with unquestioning obedience; and if, as in this case, there were no clear rules to guide me, I could invent new rules for myself, just to make sure that I did not accidentally transgress. *Or* I could think about the rules I had been given carefully, do what was required of me, and at the same time use every way available to make the task quicker and easier.

Looking back, I saw a pattern to my childhood behaviour, and knew what I would have done a year ago. I followed rules. Not unquestioningly, perhaps; but eventually, inevitably, I did what I was told.

As a child I had acceded to my mother's hushing about the nature of my gift, even when I desperately wished to know more. From what Angharad had said, it seemed Mother had deprived me of something I needed to know; but I had never questioned that Branwen was right. After she had died, I had let Father go after the beast, despite knowing that nothing good would ever come of his finding it. There were spells and charms I could have used to soothe and placate him, but I had let him do what I knew what wrong, because it never occurred to me to stand up to him.

Later, when I had awoken in the cart with John, I had done what was expected of me and obeyed my father's wish that I go to my aunt. If I had not done this, if I had just *thought*, I could have talked to Angharad much earlier. And when Rother and Isolde had come to Aunt Erian's house to take me back, I had simply accepted that I must go with them, even though it meant leaving behind someone so precious to me. I squeezed my eyes shut against the prickle of tears. Yes, the last event had been influenced by Zella's spells, but if I had only struggled, questioned...

I looked down at my hand. How long would it take me to knit the tunics if I had to do it with hands like hams? Each day that went by, Zella drained more life from the Kingdom. Each day, my brothers were trapped, Ancestors knew where, between this world and the next.

That settled it.

Decision made, I closed my eyes and reached into the air around me for the enaid. It swirled and broke over me and I absorbed it, carefully feeding it into my hand. It is more difficult to heal yourself than another, for no one can see inside their own body; and sometimes, if you are tired or badly hurt, the effort it takes is more harmful than the injury itself. But Midland helped me along, and soon I looked down on a freckled hand that showed no signs of swelling or redness. For the first time I noticed that my work-worn hands had a certain beauty of their own. I smiled at the thought and got up, startling the birds on the windowsill into flight.

I washed in the icy water from the well, dressed, combed and rebraided my hair and breakfasted well on what was left of my supper from last night, thinking all the while about the task I had to complete. I looked thoughtfully at the leather sacks I had brought with me. My hands were small enough that I believed I could make myself a pair of gloves from one of them. Much better than collecting the wanton's needle entirely unprotected. I emptied both bags and found the small wooden box containing two fine needles and several reels of thread which Olwyn had given me. Then I got out my knife and began hacking away at one of the bags.

It took me several hours, and by the time I was finished I was beginning to wonder if it was even worth it, I had stabbed myself so many times. I thanked the Ancestors that the leather was worn so thin and soft, or I should never have managed to get a needle through it at all. The result was far from pretty, and resembled mittens more than gloves. I wouldn't be able to strip, knot or weave the nettles in them, but they would do for harvesting the plant. I tied the gloves carefully to the girdle of my dress with a leftover bit of leather.

Then I took the other empty pack and hitched it over my shoulder, setting out to look for lady's hook, ammemnon flowers and redroot. These plants, when steeped in hot water, drained and mashed together, formed a powerful salve which Mother had applied to nasty burns. The sweet-smelling medicine stopped blistering and numbed the skin – just the thing I needed to help me work swiftly on my brothers' tunics.

At this time of year lady's hook and redroot were easily found, but the tiny yellow ammemnon flowers were more common in the Kingdom than Midland – again I missed Gabriel, who I knew would have been able to tell me just where to look – and so the rest of the morning had passed before I returned home and began mixing up the salve. I had no bowls to store it in, but Olwyn had left one of the jars of pickled vegetables in my pack, and the thick, rippled glass was miraculously unshattered. It would mean eating nothing but the jar's contents for my midday meal to avoid waste – not a task I relished – but the solid, sealed container was worth it. I tied the herbs I did not use with strips of petticoat and hung them from the ceiling to dry. While preparing the plants and mashing them, I channelled every charm for healing, soothing, cooling and renewing that I could think of, hoping they would infuse the salve and make it more effective. By early afternoon the salve, an unpleasant greeny-brown colour, was ready. I scraped as much of the mixture as I could into the little box which had held the needles and thread and put it into the remaining leather sack. Then I went out to gather wanton's needle.

I had a good sheaf of the accursed things when I headed home, and several stings on my forearms. The spines of the nettle sank deep into my skin if I so much as brushed them, and the gloves were too short. I had no more leather to make gauntlets, so I would simply have to be careful. Despite the heat I put more of the swept-out rubbish into the fire and took the nettles and hung them, tied with the last of the petticoat strips, from the mantelpiece, so that they would dry more quickly.

By evening I was ready to begin stripping them into their individual tough strands of flax. I had to take my gloves off for this, but luckily the heat had crisped the spines so that most of them could no longer stick into my skin. Less luckily, the fibrous stuff of the nettles was razor-sharp. My hands were soon criss-crossed with fine bloody lines.

After some experimenting, I found that I could braid several pieces together, and then tie two more braids to the top and bottom of the first, and another between the second two, to make a square frame, within which I could weave more pieces of the nettle flax. These squares could then be sewn together with some of the finer strands to create flat panels, and the flat panels would become tunics. It was not a pretty, skilful form of constructing the tunics, but for someone who had never trained as a weaver, it was quick and relatively easy.

I was constrained by the size of the nettles themselves as to how large I could make these squares; wanton's needle was not a tall plant, and so the strands of flax were not long enough to make any square bigger than the span of my hand. It would take at least ten squares to make the front of one tunic and if I was to give each tunic sleeves, which I reasoned it was best to do, then it would take more than two dozen squares to make each tunic. It took me that whole first evening to get halfway through the first square.

By the time I finished my evening's work, my skin was beginning to throb and blister. I washed my burning hands in well water and sat down with one of my needles to laboriously pick out the few spines which had escaped the heat of the fire. Finally I applied more of the salve. I dared not use too much enaid, because, like all things, charms if used too often lose their effectiveness, and I did not want to develop a resistance to my own spells. So when the pain in my skin was reduced to a sullen throb, I had to be content.

Over the following weeks, I grew adept at drying the confounded nettles quickly, at stripping them into flax, and at knotting and twisting and braiding them. I also grew adept at digging the spines from my hands, bandaging the cuts from the flax with tiny strips of cloth, and mixing up greater and greater quantities of salve. The moon waxed, waned, waxed and waned again, and summer's heat began to make the nights in the cottage unpleasantly humid. In time, my fears about my own resistance to magic proved true. Despite my sparing use of them, the small charms became ineffective, and the salve and gloves were the only protection I had.

Once the charms stopped working, the combination of blisters, swelling and cuts soon created unpleasant scarring, especially on my fingers, which gave them the claw-like look of advanced age. The scars were dead to all but the most extreme pains, and so their cushioning presence on my fingers actually made knitting the tunics easier. But the masses of scar tissue lessened my fingers' mobility, causing most other tasks to become more difficult.

One of my greatest unhappinesses in those days was that I could not make the progress I wished on the tunics. I had to forage for all the food I ate, for windfall firewood and kindling since I had no axe, and I had to keep the cottage clean and my own single dress and cloak in good repair. In order to reduce the time spent looking for food, I devoted a few days to clearing out the kitchen garden and the herb patch, and they provided some staples for my diet. Nevertheless, I still had much less time to devote to the tunics than I wished. I found that my rate had stabilized at about two squares a week and rarely did I manage more than that. I chafed at my own slowness, and at the thought of all the long weeks ahead.

As the blackberries ripened on their thorny bushes, I finished the first tunic. It had taken me sixteen weeks to complete, and as I looked at it, I had to tense all my muscles to stop myself from flinging it into the fire.

Sometimes I thought I saw swans in the sky. I might glimpse a flash of snowy white through the trees, or a reflection of bright black eyes in the well as I leaned over it. Sometimes I dreamed of my brothers, but never in their human form. They always came to me as great white birds. And though occasionally I heard their voices, their words carried haunting echoes of lapping water, rushing wind and the music of wingbeats, so that at times I could barely understand them.

Whether these things were real or mere imagination I had no idea. I had no idea if the visions should offer me comfort or despair. I liked to think that my brothers were with me. But it was their human faces that I yearned to see, and I didn't know if I ever would again.

And yet, even as I worried and fretted about my brothers' fate, other thoughts refused to leave my mind. Despite my own stern, internal lectures, despite knowing I would probably never see him again, I could not get Gabriel out of my head. Sometimes I thought I was going a little insane with my longing for his company, his voice ... his touch.

One evening I dozed off by the fire and dreamed of him riding on a pale horse through a forest very like my own, in the twilight. He was alone, and his face was sad. It hurt me to look at him when he was not smiling, but I could not tear my dreaming eyes away. I woke to a strange restlessness, a hot, achy feeling in my body that lasted all morning, and then subsided into listlessness for the rest of the day.

Another time I saw him leaning on battlements of white stone, staring into the night sky, his expression pensive. I watched his hair ruffle in the brisk wind and, in the dream, reached out to touch him. For a moment it was as if the dream was real – he stiffened at my tentative hand on his shoulder and whirled round, shock and joy on his face. But his eyes looked through me until the happiness faded from them, and after a while he turned away again with a muffled groan, kicking the stone wall before him. When I got up that day I accidentally dropped a bunch of my painstakingly dried herbs into the fire, and then spent half an hour crying into my skirt before I pulled myself together.

One night I had a dream of phantom hands – familiar hands – stroking gently over my body. Of the moistness of lips and tongue, the warmth of breath on my skin, and the sharp, playful nip of teeth. I woke sobbing, and from then on my sleep was light and restless. Perhaps I did not trust myself to dream.

On a slightly frosty morning I woke from my restless

slumber shivering under my spread cloak to find that I had allowed my store of dried nettles to become low. Not stopping for breakfast, I took up my pack and went out to harvest more wanton's needle.

My cheeks tingled with the snapping air as I travelled along the now well-walked trail through the trees, kicking up fallen leaves and stamping my feet to rid them of the cold. Since an unfortunate incident with some curious pine martens who had tried to nest in the cottage, I carried the completed and half-finished tunics with me whenever I left the house; and they cushioned my back against the sharp edges of the salve box as the sack bounced on my shoulders.

A morning of hard work cutting the nettles banished the remains of the chill, and I was in quite good humour as I sat on a rocky boulder at the edge of the granite escarpment and rubbed salve into my smarting forearms. I was so used to the sensation by now that it hardly consumed any of my attention – which is why I heard the distant call of the hunting horn so clearly on the still autumn air.

I froze, fingers ceasing their familiar movement. Nothing. Had I imagined it?

Just as I was about to dismiss the noise as nothing more than a figment of my imagination, the horn rang out again. Its rich, deep tone was closer this time – and in its wake I could now make out, very faintly, the belling of hounds.

A hunting party.

In all the months I had inhabited this patch of forest I had not seen so much as the shadow of another human being, nor heard a human voice. The thought of other people, – *strangers* – filled me with an odd, panicky sense of fear. My months of isolation had changed me. I could not bear to face others now, tatty and mute and scarred as I was. I wasn't ready! I *couldn't* see anyone.

I'll go back to the cottage; they won't mind me.

But as stood, another feeling tugged at the back of my mind. It was familiar and yet strange – like the sensation of welcome I had felt when I first arrived in Midland, but also like the disturbing feelings that had sometimes upset my dreams so badly. I thought I heard the rushing sea and the keening cries of seagulls. Something – someone – called out to me, not with curiosity, but with recognition.

The touch of that presence held me in place even as I strained against its claim on me. Torn between the equally strong desires to run and to stay, I hesitated too long.

Hounds broke through the trees and streamed around me, their brown and white speckled bodies wriggling with delight as they greeted me. I heard the crashing of undergrowth as the riders followed them and pushed the dogs away frantically.

No, no! I told them, head swivelling as I pushed my way through their furry mass, avoiding a dozen eager tongues. *Your people aren't hunting for me – you're supposed to be sniffing out bears or stags. Go away!*

The dogs persisted, one very large one going so far as to leap up and place his large muddy paws on my shoulders to swipe my face with his tongue.

They *were* looking for me, the big dog said. The others agreed in chorus as he continued. The pack *had* been looking for wild boar, but just now Dog-Master-Man had changed his mind and given them her scent instead, and so they had found her. Dog-Master-Man would be so pleased with them! He would scratch them behind their ears and tickle their stomachs.

I gave up. It was too late to make it back to the cottage now. I pushed the big dog off me and jumped up onto the first rocky ledge on the granite cliff, climbing to its peak with fear-born speed. I huddled down, hoping the dull green of my dress would fade into the vegetation. The crown of saplings certainly masked my sight; apart from brief glimpses as the leaves caught the wind, I could only listen to what was happening below.

I heard the deep pounding of hooves as the riders broke through into the clearing, and the frighteningly alien sound of human voices. I was too far up to make out their words, but tone I could distinguish. Two hunters calling to each other, and a lighter voice belonging to a woman, answering them with amusement. The horn rang out again as the horses stamped and snorted. I huddled deeper, longing for them to be gone.

Then I heard a new voice. It was different from the others, lower, filled with authority and bringing with it the quiet echo of familiarity that had tugged at me before. Unconsciously I tensed, coming up onto my knees and leaning forward through the trees. I knew that voice. It was impossible ... but I knew it.

I couldn't see anything. I leaned forward still more, craning sideways to try to catch a glimpse of the speaker below.

Then I heard the voice again, this time raised in a shout. "Alexandra! *Alexandra!*"

Stunned recognition hit me.

My fingers slid off the damp moss and I skidded forward on my knees, teetering on the top of the cliff. I could have caught myself – except for a suddenly vivid memory of the hundreds of gently waving wanton's needle below, and the intense wish to avoid peppering my whole body with their stings.

So I threw myself backwards, remembering a moment too late that the drop on the other side was a sheer one. I flipped over the edge, plummeting straight down. There was a blinding flare of pain across my forehead as I glanced off something sharp, followed abruptly by darkness.

CHAPTER
FIFTEEN

Sensations swam up through the darkness slowly. First came a pleasant, herby scent, mixed with the smell of freshly laundered linen. There was coolness on my head, followed by a nasty ache. The pain pushed down on my floating consciousness, flattening me with such enthusiasm that I finally woke up in protest.

The first thing I saw was sunlight, filtering in thin, silky ribbons through a pierced marble screen before a trio of arched windows to my right. The wall was smooth, white stone. I turned my head, and found myself staring up at a vaulted ceiling, carved in the same white stone. Little faces smiled or leered down at me from the cornices.

I was lying on a huge raised wooden bed. The counterpane under my body was the palest shade of blushing rose, so soft and smooth that even my crabbed fingers couldn't snag it. I blinked blurrily, and raised a hand to the dull throb of my head. My fingers met a pulpy coolness, and I pulled it away to see a herb poultice – ragwort and flowering ester. Deprived of the soothing coolness, my forehead thudded with warning pain as I lifted my other hand and gingerly explored the area. I could feel a tender bump on my hairline and broken skin. Someone had washed the blood away; my hair still felt damp.

What had happened, and where was I?

There was a rustle to my left. I tensed, and felt a sharp twinge as my head responded.

"Hush now."

The light, warm voice belonged to a woman. Before I could find the energy to turn my head, I heard the scrape of chair legs on stone, and a figure dressed in deep rose wool appeared at my side. Her pretty face showed the lines of a woman in her late forties, but her long black hair, pulled back to tumble over her shoulders, held no more than a gleam of silver.

She smiled reassuringly, and her grey eyes showed compassion and friendliness. "There's no need to panic. You're with friends now." She sat down beside me on the bed, her voice a soothing murmur. "My son tells me you're called Alexandra, from Farland. I'm Rose, and I'm a cunning woman too – though not as good as you are, if my son's stories are anything to go by. Do you mind if I look at your head?"

I shook my head, then winced as my vision swam dizzily.

"There now." She touched my brow lightly, and I felt a gentle flow of warmth – her gift, scented with roses and the patter of cool rain – settle into the throbbing hurt, easing away the worst of the pain. "You had a nasty fall. Just let me look after you." A momentary pause. "Hmm. Well, the ester's taken down the swelling, but this is still a raw cut. I'll put on some more ragwort to help it along." Delicious coolness as she daubed on the sharp-smelling ointment.

I sighed silently, then opened my eyes again to meet hers as she hovered over me.

"Do you think you might sit up? There's someone outside who's pacing a runnel in the flagstones waiting to hear you're well."

I nodded, very gently, and let her help me into a sitting position. Her voice – was this pillow too thick? I must say if I felt uncomfortable – washed over me as she tucked pillows behind my back and made me comfortable, before walking to the door and pulling it open.

From the moment I had seen my healer's grey eyes – no, from the moment I had woken – I had been expecting this. But when the familiar figure stepped into the room, I still felt as if the sea was thundering in my chest.

His shoulders had broadened, and he must have grown half a foot. He was browner. But his dark hair, untousled by the sea wind, still curled stubbornly at the ends and the smattering of golden freckles decorated the bridge of his nose as always. He had changed so much, and yet he was just as I remembered him, just as I had dreamed him. I met his steady silver gaze and felt my lips curve into a grin of pure happiness. *Gabriel.*

The next moment he was across the room and his arms were around me, hugging me fiercely. I breathed in as I buried my face in his shoulder, inhaling lye soap and his own warm scent. Oh, to be *held* again, oh Ancestors, to touch him again... I wanted to weep in his arms at the sheer joy of that embrace. But I couldn't.

The awareness forced me to let go before I broke.

Gabriel pulled back reluctantly, leaving his hands on my shoulders. "Alexandra," he murmured, staring at me as if he could hardly believe his own eyes. "I waited for you on the beach every night for hours, until Anne came to tell me you had gone. Even when we came back here I kept thinking I could ... could *feel* you, just around the corner. I dreamed about you." He flushed.

Me too, *me too*... I longed to say the words. I met his eyes and nodded.

He flushed more deeply. "When I sensed you in the forest, I thought I was going mad. But the dogs felt it too, so I sent them after the feeling, never really believing... Dear Ancestors, Alexandra! What happened to you? Where have you *been*? Talk to me!"

I stared back at him, and silently shook my head.

He frowned. "Alexandra?"

"Her head is probably buzzing," said Rose, who had kept her place by the door. "What with my gabbling and now yours, she hasn't been able to say a word since she woke up."

Something must have shown in my eyes. Gabriel's expression turned grave. Without taking his hands from my shoulders, he twisted his head to look at Rose. "She hasn't said anything, Mother? Not a word?"

"Why ... no. She's only just awakened, and she must be feeling ill." Rose stopped abruptly, perhaps struck by the realization that she was speaking for me again.

"I don't think that's why she hasn't spoken." He turned back to look at me and asked quietly, "What's wrong, sweetheart?"

I bit my lip. Then I raised a hand – hidden in a fold of my sleeve, so that only my fingertips showed – to my throat and shook my head.

He swallowed. "You can't talk?"

I shook my head again.

"Is this ... something to do with why you were living all alone in the woods?" he asked.

I nodded hesitantly.

There was a long pause. Then he said, "They never came, did they?"

I knew whom he meant. My lips quirked as I shook my head again.

"Are you in some kind of trouble?"

How on earth could I possibly explain? I tilted my head and shrugged helplessly. *Sort of.*

Rose came closer, looking thoughtful.

"There's no scarring on Alexandra's throat, and I sensed no injury there when I reached into her. I did sense one of the strongest – perhaps *the* strongest – healing affinities I've ever come across. There's something ... I don't know. I think this silence may be part of an enchantment, a very powerful healing spell."

I nodded at Gabriel, then smiled at Rose gratefully. She smiled back, her eyes twinkling wryly. Then a considering look crossed her face, and she turned from us and stooped down beside the bed. When she stood back up, she held in her hands a very familiar, battered leather pack. "Perhaps this is part of it?"

Of course. It had been on my shoulders when I climbed the granite cliff. With mixed feelings of relief and guilt – for I had completely forgotten it – I took the pack. I opened the fastening and pulled out the fresh nettles, barely feeling the stings on my calloused hands as I rummaged to make sure that the finished and half-finished tunics were still there. I found them safe at the bottom, and relaxed.

I looked back up to see Gabriel staring at my exposed hands in horror. "What have you done to yourself?" he cried, grabbing my left hand and examining it. The purplish ripples of scar tissue stood out lividly. I felt my face burning and tried to tug my hand away, but he held fast.

Rose was staring with wide eyes at the nettle tunics, half pulled from the sack. "Ancestors. I think Alexandra has answered our question. Let me see." Reluctantly I yielded up my hand to her. My fingers had curled into a fist of embarrassment, but she carefully unfolded them, examining the scars. Then she returned my hand to my lap and looked at the nettles spilled over my skirt.

"These are wanton's needle. It's a horrible nettle – its sting makes the flesh swell and burn. And these..." She wrapped her fingers in the edge of her sleeve and picked up one of the tunics. "You're using the nettles to make clothes. One tunic, one half done." She looked at me thoughtfully. "Hmm..."

"Will you please tell me what this is about, Mother?" Gabriel demanded.

"I'm afraid I can't. It tugs at an old memory – perhaps something in one of my books. There's definitely some kind of spell here, but that's all I can say."

He took one of my crabbed, bent hands in his and held it, nursing it like a wounded bird as he looked at me. "Why did you do this to yourself? Weaving with nettles – why?"

I looked at him in appeal, biting my lip, and shook my head. *Please don't ask more. How can I explain if I can't speak?*

He met my eyes for a moment, and then his gaze dropped. "All right. I'm sorry. I'm sure that whatever you do must be for a good reason." I arched my brow at that, and won a small smile from him. Then he sighed. "If you must do this ... well, wanton's needle grows plentifully enough near by. Won't you stay here, with us? I can send people to fetch anything you want from the forest – I'll help you in any way I can."

I smiled at him gladly and nodded my agreement, but inside there was an ache of sadness. My muteness had not bothered me while I lived in the woods; but now I was with Gabriel, the one person in the world whom I needed and wanted to talk to – and I could not utter a word.

With a determined look, I conveyed to them both I wanted to leave the room and look around. Tomorrow I would need to get back to work, but it couldn't hurt to take one day to explore Gabriel's home. I still had no idea where I was. Rose and Gabriel exchanged a glance, perhaps worried about my head, but I persisted, and eventually Rose opened the door, while Gabriel took my arm to lead me out.

"Er, there's something I should have told you before now, Alexandra," he began as we stepped into a long, white corridor. The only colour was in the lush rugs underfoot, and I was looking at the intricate patterns rather than listening to him as he continued. "It didn't seem to matter at the time, but..."

Before he could finish his sentence, a small man, dressed elaborately in purple satin, came round the corner. When he saw Gabriel and Rose, he stopped abruptly. He gave my bedraggled appearance one surprised look, then turned away.

"Your Lordship." He bowed deeply to Gabriel. "My Lady," he murmured reverently to Rose, who nodded at him. "I was looking for you to ask..."

I didn't listen to the rest of the man's sentence but turned shocked eyes on Gabriel. *Your Lordship?*

"Yes, I'm afraid so," he whispered. "I'm sorry I didn't tell you before, but I didn't think of it the first time we met and afterwards it would have seemed like boasting. 'Oh, by the way, I'm heir to the principality of Midland and my father's the prince.'" Seeing my eyes widen even more at this casual disclosure, he added anxiously, "You're not upset, are you? I didn't mean to deceive you."

I let out a long breath and then shook my head. I only wished it were possible for me to explain the truth about my identity. There were so many things I wanted to say to Gabriel, so many secrets I longed to share, but while my task bound me...

I could never tell him how I felt.

CHAPTER
SIXTEEN

Before any more could be said, a deep peal rang out over our heads, making me jump.

Gabriel explained, "It's the supper bell. The food will be ready in an hour; I don't think we have time to explore after all. But you will eat with us, won't you?"

I glanced down at my shabby, patched, faded and fraying dress, and then looked at Rose helplessly.

She laughed. "Oh, poor Alexandra!"

"I don't understand," said Gabriel, puzzled.

"She has nothing to wear."

His confused expression did not change.

"Never mind, my son," Rose said. "Go up to your rooms and get ready for the meal, and I shall arrange a bath for Alexandra and find her some clothes."

I luxuriated in the copper bathing tub, washing myself with real, beautifully perfumed soap, and letting Rose massage shampoo into my tangled hair.

"I've never seen such hair," she muttered to herself. Whether this was curse or compliment I did not know.

The water was an alarming greyish colour by the time I was finished; my hasty wahes in the chilly water from the well obviously had not been as thorough as I had hoped.

Hauled out and dried off, my hair combed until it rose up in a thick, crackling red cloud, I wass left alone as Rose went in search of a gown that might fit me. I must have grown again – I towered over Rose – so none of her things would do. I thought wistfully of the trunks of beautiful dresses that had gone with Isolde and Rother back to the Kingdom. I wondered what Zella had done with them. Shredded them in rage? Probably. They wouldn't suit her, that was certain.

I pulled out the half-finished tunic while I waited for Rose to come back, and occupied myself with stripping that morning's nettles. I had stopped to pick the stings out and rub salve into my hands when Rose came back, face triumphant. She had a swathe of vibrant kingfisher-blue fabric over her arm, which she shook out to reveal a gown.

"I almost had to prise this from Lady Suttel's hands. But it would have suited her very ill anyway," she said. "She is dark, you know. Dark-haired ladies look sallow in blue. It will look wonderful on you. Come on."

She put a shift of soft white muslin over my head, then the dress itself, laced the tight bodice of the gown down my front, and stood back to admire the result. The dress seemed to fit me very well indeed, though the tight sleeves were a little long. I looked down and saw that its low, round neckline exposed an alarmingly large amount of bosom, which I'd never realized I had before. My hands flew up to cover it. The gowns my aunt had made for me never looked like this!

"Now, now, there's no need for that," Rose said, pulling my hands away. "You look lovely. This is the latest fashion! As for your hair..."

I reached back with the swiftness of long practice, caught my hair and braided it tightly, twisting it into its customary heavy knot at the nape of my neck.

"Oh no," Rose said, coming behind me and unravelling my hair just as swiftly as I'd plaited it. "No one has worn their hair like that for twenty years! Just let me..." With a few twists she pulled back the front and top waves of my hair and braided them, leaving the rest to cascade over my shoulders.

I looked down again at my chest, and found myself hunching over, as if to conceal the excess flesh. But bending only made it bulge, and I straightened hurriedly. I pulled the curling mass of my hair forward and arranged it to cover the low neckline. The results were not entirely satisfactory.

Rose watched my efforts with amusement. "You'll draw more attention to yourself that way," she said. I glared at her, and she burst out laughing.

Just then another thunderous peal of sound broke over us, and I jumped again.

"Our meal will be ready in a few minutes. It's time for us to go down, and for everyone to see you."

I gave her a quizzical glance. Her smile was decidedly smug. "Just wait."

She led me from the room, in the opposite direction to earlier. We turned a corner and the passage opened out onto a little balcony. The sun had almost set, but there was enough light to illuminate the scene below, and I stopped dead.

It was the city. The great city of Midland that had once been called the City of Flowers. Spread out before me in an immense sweep, it was a jumble of twinkling lights, sharp silhouettes of white and grey stone houses, and winding roads, stretching into the distance.

I had failed to make the connection between Gabriel and Rose being Midland's heir and lady, and the place where Midland's prince – and his family – must live. Good Ancestors! In my little cottage in the woods, I could have been no more than half a day's ride from the city – and Gabriel – for all those months.

This place, this building where I stood, must be the glimmering pearly spike I had seen on my journey with John. I leaned over the edge of the balcony and let myself stare. From afar it had seemed awesome. This close it was unbelievable.

"Have you never seen the city before?" Rose asked, after allowing me a moment to gawp.

I held up one finger, then jerked my head and made a sweeping gesture with my hand.

"You've seen it once, but never this close?" she interpreted. "I know how you feel. I can still remember the sensation of awe – almost fear – I felt when I first came here. I'd never been more than a mile from my village, but the old Prince, my husband's father, was so ill, they'd called in healers from all over Midland. Idiots. It only took me a day to realize he had pink-spot fever, and a week to make him better. But I never left." She looked at me speculatively. "Do you think it's beautiful?"

I nodded feelingly. Then I became aware that leaning over the balcony was making my chest bulge in a most alarming fashion, and jerked upright. Rose laughed at my expression and took my arm. "I'll have Gabriel show you around the place tomorrow. But we must go down now – they won't start eating until I arrive."

We walked swiftly along another corridor until we came to the head of some smooth white stairs. The sound of many voices all talking and laughing at once drifted up from somewhere below. The steps swept away to the left and out of sight around a curving wall in a fashion I had never seen before. I stared at them curiously.

"They're for making a grand entrance," Rose said. "Would you go down ahead of me, dear? I like to cling to the banister myself."

I looked at her askance, but she made a shooing gesture, and since I could not ask what she meant, I took a deep breath, shoved the thought of all those strangers out of my mind, and walked down the steps and around the curve of the wall.

I found myself stranded conspicuously on a great sweep of stairs above a gigantic banqueting hall. The ceiling arched up in great gilded stone ribs above me, interspaced with high arched windows through which the stars glittered frostily. The far wall was a screen of stone no thicker than an inch, worked and pierced as intricately as lace, allowing the evening breeze to perfume the hall. Brilliantly dyed and embroidered banners hung from the ceiling and walls into the sea of people sat at long tables below.

There must have been at least a hundred people down there. Servants scurried between the tables with jugs of wine so large they took two to carry them. The noise of talking, laughing, shouting – even some singing – was incredible. I turned my head to look back along the curve of the steps. Rose was nowhere in sight.

I was *not* going down there on my own. I gathered up a handful of my full skirts and half turned, intending to run back and find Rose. But before I could take the first step I became aware of a change in the noise below. The clamour was dying down, the chattering voices falling quiet, the laughter fading, until, with remarkable swiftness, complete silence had fallen over the great hall.

Slowly, I turned my head and looked down.

They were all staring at me. Every face was tilted up; every pair of eyes was fixed on the blue and red figure that marred their shining white stairs – even the servants were gawking, stopped in mid-trot between the tables. I froze, not daring to move a muscle, even as my mind whirled feverishly. Why did they stare so? What was wrong with me, other than the gaping neckline of the gown? Had I somehow committed some dreadful mistake without realizing it? Why were they *staring*?

The stillness of the scene was broken by a quick movement from the shortest table in the room, which stood on a raised dais to my left. It was Gabriel, pushing himself up from his seat, leaping off the dais and striding to the foot of the stairs. He was grinning, obviously waiting for me to walk down to him.

The look of pleasure and welcome on his face was enough to break my paralysis. I took a deep breath, straightened my shoulders, removed the hand that had unconsciously crept up to cover my chest, and caught hold of my skirts firmly. Then, with every ounce of dignity I possessed, I slowly walked down the painfully long curve of the stairs into the hall.

Somewhat to my own surprise, I reached the bottom without tripping over my dress, but I was still pricklingly conscious of the dozens of pairs of eyes riveted on me. I kept my gaze firmly on Gabriel as I stepped down onto the pink-veined marble of the floor. His grey eyes shone, and I felt a surge of happiness in response. My awareness of the others in the hall faded away. Let them stare, I thought fuzzily. I don't care.

He reached out to take my hand, untangling it from my skirts. His palm closed around mine, and slowly he raised my crabbed, twisted fingers to his lips, and pressed a kiss to them.

"You're so lovely," he said, as if in answer to a question. "They stare because you're so lovely."

I blinked at him, a dozen protests automatically rising to my lips and just as automatically bitten back. Suddenly I was grateful that I could not speak, and had no duty to deny his words. I just smiled back.

A deafening cheer went up from the crowded tables. Everyone in the hall was on their feet, stamping and clapping, whistling, waving fists in the air. I gave Gabriel an alarmed look. What was happening now?

He rolled his eyes apologetically. "They get a bit carried away at times," he said.

I felt heat rising in my cheeks. I'd forgotten anyone was even in the hall with us.

Gabriel held up his hands in a gesture for silence. "Yes! Thank you!" he bellowed. "Quiet, if you please!"

The cheering died down amid much laughter and scraping as people retook their seats. Rose came bouncing down the stairs to stand beside us. She was a little flushed, as if she might have been laughing, but she returned my accusing glare with bland innocence.

"I realized I had forgotten something," she said airily. "But you seem to have managed. Shall we be seated? I'm sure we're all famished by now."

She led the way to the dais and up the two shallow steps to the fine table where the Prince and his family obviously dined. The larger, throne-like chair in the middle was obviously hers, which was a relief. I didn't think I could have eaten with Gabriel sitting next to me.

As we sat, the sound of the gong rang out again. "Oh dear, we have kept them waiting," Rose said. "They're impatient."

Sure enough, within moments, a horde of servants bubbled out of a door to our left, bringing with them delicious smells. They bore giant black cauldrons and silver platters, spreading through the hall to serve the evening meal. One of the cauldrons was brought to the centre of our table, where its lid was lifted to reveal a savoury mixture of potatoes, cabbage, mushrooms and cheese, mashed together and fried. The smell made my mouth water. It was followed by thick, lavishly buttered slabs of bread, baked potatoes filled with cheese and meat or fruit, and by giant trenchers of roasted meat. There were a dozen different vegetables, all dripping with butter. Even for one who ate no meat, there was a surplus of choice. It took all my discipline to stop myself diving on my plate, and I knew even then that I was eating too quickly for politeness. I had not eaten so well since I left the Hall.

I saw Rose eyeing me as my plate emptied; before I could sit back in embarrassment, she slipped two more fried potato cakes onto my plate, added some buttery mashed swede, and passed me the bread. "You could do with a little more fat, dear," she said matter-of-factly, returning to her own meal.

After we had all eaten our fill, the servants came back and cleared away the debris. Then a minstrel played a lap harp and pipes for us with skill and enthusiasm. Several of his tunes were obviously Midland ones, for I had never heard them before, and I enjoyed the novelty. But his final song was, by some coincidence, my favourite: "The Tears of Mairid Westfield". I found my throat working, though no noise escaped my lips, as the hall filled with voices.

"*The tears of Mairid Westfield*
Could have drowned the starry sky.
The tears of Mairid Westfield
Were her sorrowful goodbye;
For though she gave the warning
Her love returned too late;
And the tears of Mairid Westfield
Could not change her woeful fate."

At last, replete and sleepy, the people began to trickle from the hall. Rose yawned delicately and excused herself, waving away Gabriel's polite offer to escort her to her rooms. "You're both young enough to enjoy a lazy autumn evening. If Alexandra feels well, why don't you take her for a walk in the gardens? Show her my flowers."

I felt my face burning again at her tone. Gabriel grinned at me and said pointedly, "Goodnight, Mother."

"Goodnight." She winked at both of us. I wanted to cover my face with my hands, but contented myself with giving her another stern look, which she avoided by leaving.

Gabriel claimed my hand, tugging me to my feet. "Would you like to walk in the gardens? They're lovely at this time of year." He added invitingly, "Mother has imported flowers from all over the continent."

I hesitated, tempted, then nodded. I was surprised when, instead of leading me towards one of the doors, he went to the far wall, gripped a handle hidden in the fretwork and folded back a section of the stone screen on invisible hinges. The opening led onto a stone-paved terrace, where miniature trees, trained into cone and sphere shapes, grew in brass pots. Their tiny white flowers perfumed the air with a sweet musky scent, rather like night-blooming jasmine. My eyes adjusted quickly to the shadows as Gabriel turned back to close the screen door behind him, and I let my gaze travel upwards to the towering white heights of the palace, smudgy now in the shadows. A black vine rioted over the side of the building, even making it so far as the battlements from which the great tower sprouted. I thought of the damage such a voracious plant would do to a wattle and daub Kingdom house, and shuddered. Why did no one check its unrestrained growth? I touched Gabriel's arm and pointed to the nearest snarl of black thorns, raising my eyebrows questioningly.

"You want to know about the prince's rose?" he asked.

I felt my eyebrows shoot up still further. Rose? I reached out to touch one of the withered-looking, blackish-purple leaves. It looked like no rose I'd ever seen.

He took my arm and together we began to walk along the terrace. Dimly in the twilight, I could see the rest of the gardens spreading away beneath us in a series of stacked terraces. They looked like the gently curving inner layers of a shell. As I glanced up at the night sky, I saw three white shapes flitting across the clouds, and was comforted. My brothers were here.

"The prince's rose is probably the most interesting plant in the gardens," he began. "The story says that it was planted by Prince Aelred – the first true prince of Midland, who was granted the lands here after the Long War – when he built this palace nearly eight hundred years ago. Anyway, the rose was supposed to be incredibly beautiful. Golden, with an intoxicating scent. Apparently it bloomed almost constantly during his reign and continued to do so during our times of peace; half the palace was covered with it, and the books say that it looked as if the building were gilded."

He looked at me. "Do you know much of the history of the civil wars in Midland?" he asked.

I tilted my head from side to side and waved a hand. *A little.*

He understood, and continued. "The wars started more than a hundred years ago, when Prince Anders died without a direct heir. He chose one of his nephews to succeed him, but unfortunately, just after the prince died, the heir was murdered by poison. There's a legend that a woman started the fighting – a beautiful woman, naturally – by bewitching the brother of the chosen heir and getting it into his head that he should be Prince instead. So he killed his brother with a potion this woman gave him, and then his other brothers turned on him, and their cousins joined in, and everything went mad for a good long while. History calls the woman a witch but, whoever she was, things didn't go her way, because the man she'd enchanted was unexpectedly killed in battle and his own men turned on her and drove her away. It's said she turned into a wolf or a grey fox as she fled, and that the blood of the battlefield stained her pelt red. A nice story."

A strange shiver went down my spine. A beautiful woman, adept with poisons, who turned into a wolf-like creature with bloody red fur?

"What is it?" Gabriel asked, concerned. I'd stopped walking. I gestured that I was fine. He looked unconvinced. "Is your head paining you? We could go back in."

I shook my head and managed a smile, motioning for him to continue. With reluctance, he began walking again, and took up the tale.

"Well, it's said that as soon as the first drop of blood was spilled, the prince's rose stopped blooming; the flowers withered away. They've never bloomed since. But we leave the vine to grow out of respect for our ancestor who planted it."

I was barely listening to him now. Instead I saw a wolf-like creature, stained red with blood, crawling away into the forests of the Kingdom to lick its wounds. I knew Zella was older than she looked. Was she over a hundred years old?

"Alexandra?" Gabriel's voice interrupted my confusion.

I'd stopped walking again. I realized I really didn't feel well. My bruised temple was pounding, and I remembered that I had been up since dawn, picking nettles. So much had happened since then; I just wanted to sit quietly somewhere and think. Or better yet, sleep. I pulled a face in apology and shrugged.

"No, *I'm* sorry," he said remorsefully. "I should have known better. Shall I take you back to your room?"

I nodded gratefully, leaning on his arm as we went back along the terrace and through the hall. In my sudden weakness it was all I could do to make it up the grand sweep of stairs, and eventually, with a muffled exclamation he picked me up and carried me. I was too thankful to be off my feet to manage more than a token protest, which he quashed easily.

"Stop it," He said severely. "You're unwell and you weigh nothing anyway. You've not been eating properly. You weighed almost the same when I first met you, and you were a foot shorter then." He reached the top of the stairs and walked along the passage to the room where I had woken earlier. "You shouldn't have let me drag out you out into the gardens. I can be an idiot sometimes – but you're a bigger idiot if you don't point it out to me."

I laughed silently, my face hidden in his shoulder. He could not know how much comfort I drew from being looked after like this. I was very glad that no one was about to witness his display of caring, though. Judging from the reaction earlier when he had only held my hand, the tale would have been all over the palace by morning. Gabriel pushed open the door of my room without anyone seeing us.

The room was dark, but enough moonlight came through the window screen to illuminate the furniture, allowing him to place me carefully on the edge of the bed. I sat up, clasping my hands in my lap as he looked down at me.

"Shall I get a maid to come and unlace you?" he asked, his eyes going to the front of my dress.

The bodice of the dress laced along the front, where it could be easily undone and pulled off. Shamefully I remembered the last time I had dreamed of him, and felt my skin tighten and heat. I crossed my arms over my chest hurriedly so that my treacherous body could not give me away, and shook my head.

"Ahem." He cleared his throat and shuffled his feet. "Well, I'll wish you goodnight then." With an unfamiliar clumsiness, he ducked down and pressed a swift kiss on my lips. Before I could kiss him back he had turned away, framed in the doorway just as he had been when I had my first sight of him earlier that day. Then the door closed behind him, and I was left alone in the quiet.

I pressed my fingers to my lips, as if I could somehow capture the fading sensation of his kiss. Then, with a noiseless sigh, I got up and unlaced the dress, folding it and the muslin shift over a chair, smoothed my hair with one of the brushes thoughtfully laid out for me, and climbed under the crisp, fine sheets of the luxurious bed. As I lay there, I realized with a stab of guilt that I had barely spared a thought for my poor brothers all evening. Tomorrow I must make the best of my good fortune here and get to work on the nettle tunics again. If that good fortune held, it would not be long before I finished them. And then...

My thoughts faded away, and I slept.

In my dreams, I was back in the Kingdom, in the wild

fields where I had played with my brothers as a child. I lay in the golden grasses by the hawthorn hedge, and watched the clouds drift overhead. But the clouds were swans, their great wings spread so that their shadows chilled me; and when the sky darkened, it was not snow that fell down to brush my face and hands and blanket the ground, but pale feathers.

A maid woke me the next morning, bringing with her a generous pitcher of hot water for washing, and an armful of dresses – hastily altered, I gathered – for me to try on. The bustling, plump woman left me when I managed to convey that I could dress alone, and came back shortly with a tray of breakfast. I feasted on thick slabs of freshly baked – still warm! – bread with butter and honey and sweet fragrant tea.

"If you please, Miss," the woman said as she cleared away the crumbs. "The Princess asked if you'd attend her in the solar."

I nodded, picking up my leather sack with its precious nettles inside. I hoped Rose didn't have any plans for me today; I wanted to finish the square I was working on and get at least part of the way through another. Not having to search for my own food and maintain the cottage would save me a great deal of time and I intended to make the most of it.

The solar was a large, round room situated near the top of the great tower, with recessed windows in the walls and cushioned window seats. Rose was seated at one of the windows with her feet up and a book in her lap. Coloured pictures of herbs and plants filled the pages.

"Hello, my dear," she said. "I thought you might like to get some work done on your nettle clothes, and this is the most pleasant room for it."

I smiled in thanks.

"Come and sit by me." She pointed to the other end of the window seat, and I settled happily there, leaning my back against the wall. I opened my pack and pulled out the square I was working on.

My fingers busy with their accustomed task, it was a few minutes before I glanced up. Rose was not attending to her book, but looking out of the window. There was a fine view from where we sat, down into the front courtyard of the palace; I could see the glitter of a moat below, and the busy comings and goings of various carts and tradespeople across the lowered drawbridge.

I caught her eye and tilted my head in question. *What are you looking for?*

"Caught." She smiled. "My husband has been away for more than a month on a matter of state. We are expecting him back any day now. This is the best place for watching, as well as working."

Her eyes strayed back to the view, and I reached out to touch her arm in a tentative gesture of comfort.

She patted my hand. "It's only that he's been away

longer than normal. If I'd known how long his trip would take, I might have chosen to go with him. But I should have felt a hypocrite showing respect at the old fool's burning. I never liked the man much, and his recent exploits beggared belief. Marrying a slip of a girl, exiling his own children at her behest, emptying Farland's coffers to build some ridiculous pleasure palace for her, and then being pushed into an early grave by trying to keep up with the little drab, no doubt. I can't think of any man *less* deserving of respect. I only hope his children can sort out the mess he's created."

I felt the blood draining from my face as her meaning sank in. My skin turned clammy and cold and I hurriedly bent my head so that she could not see my expression. Rose's friendly chatter washed over me as I stared at the greeny-grey square pooled in my lap. I realized, with a sense of numb shame, that I was not even shocked. Some part of me had been expecting this since I had seen Zella at Olday Hill. Why would she keep the besotted king around when she was ruler in all but name? When she had managed to dominate all those who should have given him their loyalty? He could never have been more than a nuisance to her.

There was not a shred of doubt in my mind that Zella was responsible for my father's death. He had been ruddy with health before she had arrived.

I was an orphan. Perhaps I had effectively been so since

my father sent me away, but now it was true in fact as well as spirit. Involuntarily my memory reached back to an earlier time, those golden days of my early childhood, when I had been more to Father than an annoyance, when he would sweep me up in his arms and call me his sweeting. I had loved him then. But those days were so distant that they hardly seemed real. I could not even remember his smell, though I could remember taking comfort from it once. He had ignored me for far longer than he had ever loved me.

Looking back with sudden clarity, I knew that he had been a rigid man, a man who expected perfection from everyone. When he decided that I was not the daughter he wanted, I had ceased to exist for him. There was no rhyme or reason to it. There was no law that said a father must love all his children; nor one that said, if he did not, he must be evil through and through. He was just ... father. And now he was dead.

When I blinked, I was surprised to find a film of moisture in my eyes. I blinked more vigorously, and took up the nettle square again. My home rested squarely in Zella's fair hands now, and it was up to me to do something about it. I swore to the Ancestors it would not be much longer before I freed my brothers and my people.

A week passed at the palace with no sign of the prince's return. The days were filled with the comfort of Gabriel and Rose's company – and the more practical comfort of a soft warm bed and plenty of food. Just as I had hoped, my work on the tunics progressed beautifully. I did so well, in fact, that I felt no guilt during the afternoons when Gabriel showed me around his favourite parts of the palace, and took me on tours of the city. Or when I spent the best part of my evenings with Rose and Gabriel in the hall, listening to music and occasionally letting Gabriel persuade me out onto the floor into his arms, where I would try frantically to remember my long-ago dancing lessons while my heart surged against his.

It was a fine morning, surprisingly warm and bright with autumn sunlight, when the prince of Midland finally came home. I was sat on a wooden bench in the terraced gardens outside the banqueting hall, working – not entirely successfully – on a new nettle square, with Gabriel at my feet reading aloud from a book of Midland folk tales. I had been twitchy and ill at ease all morning and was hardly listening to him as I laboured over the stubborn nettles.

There was a sudden, joyous burst of noise from beyond the hall in the front courtyard of the palace: horns sounding the melody that welcomes the hunter home, and cheering and shouting. Gabriel's head came up, a grin splitting his face, and he jumped to his feet.

"It must be Father!" he cried. "At last! Come on."

He grabbed my hand and pulled me up, barely giving me time to put my work down before he had the screen open and was through it. The hall was bright and echoing at this time of day, with the long tables put away and the sunlight streaming through the high windows and the pierced stone screen. As we walked in, the door to the left of the sweeping stair-case was flung open and a man in dusty travel-stained clothes appeared. He was tall and well muscled, with curling sandy hair that was greying at the temples, and a slight smattering of freckles across the bridge of his nose. If that had not told me his identity, the grin that creased his lips would have.

"Gabriel!" he bellowed, leaping forward to embrace his son. They hugged for a long moment, slapping each other's backs vigorously. I hung back, feeling left out and still troubled by the uneasiness which had dogged me all morning. Something was hovering just beyond the reach of my awareness, making the tiny hairs on the back of my neck stand up.

"Father, I thought you were never coming home." Gabriel said, pulling away at last. "What have you been doing? Why did you send us no word?"

"You're as bad as your mother." The prince laughed – a happy, booming laugh. The sound was somehow famil-iar. I shivered.

"I've a surprise for you," he continued. "That's why I sent no word. Come on." He grabbed his son's shoulder and pulled him through the door. I hesitated, then fol-lowed slowly.

A quartet of giant carriages stood in the courtyard, laden with boxes and trunks that were being unloaded and ferried away by droves of servants. There were several men and women who looked as travel-worn as the prince, each surrounded by a cluster of family members welcoming them. They were all wearing smiles oddly similar to that of the prince, and again I felt that shiver of worry.

Rose stood in the centre of it all, directing the servants and greeting the returning members of her household as they passed. I had expected her to glow with happiness at the return of her husband, but instead she looked slightly pale and strained. Could it be that she felt this strangeness too? Her face brightened as she saw Gabriel and me step into the light, but I hung back, my unease increasing. There was something wrong with the air – a low droning that grated against my spine and made me hunch over defensively.

"There you all are!" Rose said, sounding relieved. "Maybe now you'll tell us what this surprise of yours is, Mark!"

"Of course, my dear." He complied with alacrity, stepping towards one of the grand carriages and pulling the door open with a flourish.

The drone of swarming hornets filled my ears, pressing me against the wall, and I gagged on the stench of rotting flesh. The cheerful noise and bustle of activity ceased. Every head turned; every face went blank. All eyes focused on the open door of the carriage.

CHAPTER
SEVENTEEN

In frozen disbelief I saw a tiny figure, clad in shimmering bronze, emerging from the shadows of the vehicle. Zella languidly reached out a hand to the prince, who stepped forward with doglike gratitude to take it and help her down from the carriage. She straightened and raised her free hand, flashing with rubies, to brush back a strand of gleaming chestnut hair from her temple, a curiously stately gesture for a girl who looked no older than I.

Dear Ancestors. She's grown stronger.

The breath seemed to have turned to lead in my chest, my mind filling with a desperate refrain: *not here, not now, not here, not now*... Not with all these people here – not before the tunics are finished. Not yet ... not ready. Not here ... not now... My fingers were clenching and unclenching in desperate distress. If only I'd worked faster on the tunics; if only they were finished. *Not now!* I wasn't ready.

Zella's gaze travelled slowly over the people assembled in the courtyard, her face expressionless. She had not yet seen me where I cowered against the wall, and her inspection was leisurely. She appeared to ignore the prince's eager babbling about the honour of her visit and the welcome he wished to extend, though he still held her hand clasped in his.

My eyes flicked from those clasped hands to Rose's face and then to Gabriel's, and I saw that they alone lacked the glazed eyes and vacant smiles of the others. Instead Rose looked grimly upset and Gabriel incredulous as they took in the prince's behaviour. In a tiny flash of insight, I thought, it's their gift. They're like me – like my brothers.

And they would share my brothers' fate. As obstacles to Zella's plan, which was plainly to execute the same conquest of Midland as she had the Kingdom, their lives would be worthless. The moment she saw them...

Before I could think, my feet were moving; I was away from the wall and stepping into her sight line, intercepting her attention before it could fall on my friends.

Zella's gaze fixed on me like a punch to the face. I saw her lips part in a tiny gasp of shock; and then I was caught in the black opacity of her eyes. I was pushed backwards across the courtyard as the ravening strength of her mind bored into me. Terror screamed in my head. Her will was a black, enveloping cloud of rotted hatred and anger – and hunger, the terrible hunger for death and pain.

I had to dig my heels into the flagstones to halt my involuntary retreat, frantically throwing my gift down through the ground and out into the air to anchor myself. My nails bit into my palms as I forced myself forward. One step. Then two. Another step. I fought back with every fibre of my brain, drawing power from the land and hurling it at her, each muscle in my body contracting as if I could push her back with my physical strength. I closed my eyes. Another step. On the inside of my eyelids I could see the pulsing lines of our struggle, blackness and light intertwined, writhing together like lightning and clouds.

I became aware of her hold on the people around me wavering. She was being forced to divert energy into this fight, and let them go. They were stirring, looking at us in bewilderment. Another step. And ... another... Her rage beat down on me with increased fury – pummelling, scratching, slashing, and tearing at my mind.

I tasted blood as I bit my tongue. And then – wonder of wonders – I felt something give. The darkness seemed to falter for a second. My eyes snapped open.

I stood nose to nose with her, so close I could feel her breath on my face, and shivered with revulsion at the sensation. Her lips were drawn back in a snarl over the sharp white teeth. A low growl echoed from deep in her throat.

Then, incredibly, the snarl smoothed away, the red lips forming a soft smile.

Oh no...

There was no time to dodge or brace myself. Her hand flew up in a blur of speed, smashing into my jaw. Her strength was inhuman. A back tooth shattered in an explosion of pain as I was lifted off my feet and flung through the air. I hit the ground on my side, my hip bone and ribs jarring over the uneven flagstones as I skidded, rolled and then thudded into the wall. I opened my mouth and vomited blood and tooth fragments, choking and gasping through the pain. I heard shouting, but could not identify the words or voice through the beating of blood in my ears and the mad wasp drone of Zella's suddenly released power.

My eyes streamed; sunlight rippled and refracted through the tears, blinding me as I rolled onto my back. I knew, abruptly and with utter surety, how my mother had been defeated. It was this – the pure unexpectedness of physical attack in the midst of a magical battle. Mama had been no match for it. Neither was I.

The shouting went on, somewhere out of sight. Gabriel. It was Gabriel's voice. Fear knifed through me, bringing me back to true consciousness, and I reached up, ignoring the darts of pain in ribs and arm, to scrabble at the wall until I could pull myself into a sitting position and see what was happening.

The bystanders were huddled against the wall, terrified and helpless. Opposite me I could see the prince and princess, sheltering beside one of the carriages.

Prince Mark was bleeding from an injury to his forehead and Rose was frantically trying to staunch the blood. Gabriel stood in the centre of the courtyard, hands extended before him, holding Zella back with what looked very like one of the bubble shields from Olday Hill – a flickering, iridescent globe. His shouting became intelligible at last; he was swearing ripely, his voice shaking with strain.

"No! *No!*" I heard a new voice and for a moment did not recognize it. Then I realized it was mine. Croaky, hoarse with disuse and cracking on the words, I screamed, *"Gabriel, no!"*

Zella lazily reached out a hand, penetrated the shield and touched one of her long fingers to Gabriel's forehead. The flickering bubble disappeared. He crumpled to the ground, eyes rolling back in their sockets as he convulsed on the flagstones.

I tried to get up, couldn't and instead struggled to my knees, crawling towards him. *"Robin! Hugh! David!"*

I don't know why I called them then. I didn't even know I could. But my voice boomed like thunder, carrying ripples of power with it. There was an explosion of brightness that knocked Zella to her knees. And then they were there.

Their wingbeats rocked the courtyard, nearly blowing me over as they dropped from the sky. Their form was partially that of swans, but they wavered and flickered like lightning, their great wings casting a shadow that engulfed Zella as they mobbed her. Rage and power shimmered from them, until they looked like a crackling ball of white fire. I heard her screaming, and began crawling again.

In the seconds it took me to reach Gabriel, the shudders racking his body had lessened. Now he was only shaking weakly, as if he hadn't the strength to fight the convulsions. Foam flecked the corners of his lips. Before I even touched him I knew that I did not have the strength to affect any kind of healing. My battle with Zella had taken almost all I had. I was powerless. Half whimpering, half sobbing his name, I cupped his face in my hands, fingers helplessly stroking his skin.

There was a shriek of triumph from Zella. I looked up to see a gout of red fire arch like blood from her hands. It struck the glowing light that was my brothers; in my mind I heard a shout of pain, and their brilliance flickered. The ball of fire separated into three transparent bird shapes. Their light began to fade away, and I realized that they could not retain their corporeal forms. In seconds they were gone. I could still sense them there, but they were helpless, trapped again between this world and the next and unable to intervene.

Horror filled me. I had ruined the spell that would save them. I had let Zella goad me into speech – and destroyed their chance of freedom. Now they would be trapped for ever.

Relieved of their attack, she straightened and got to her feet, smoothing her dress. A handful of red-spattered feathers fell from her fingers and instantly melted away into nothing.

I looked back down at Gabriel. The convulsions had stopped now, and he lay still, limp, his skin tinged with blue. He would be dead in minutes. My beloved. My love.

My hands fell from his face. I sat motionless, empty. Distantly I heard soft, unhurried footsteps, coming closer. They halted at Gabriel's side. I looked up into Zella's face. She studied Gabriel thoughtfully, that little smile curling her lips.

"Shame. He was pretty."

She reached out and seized my shoulder, picking me up with one hand. I hung helplessly from her fingers, my feet inches above the ground.

"I've often imagined ripping your throat out, you know," she said quietly. "But I think this will be even better."

She closed her hand over my throat and squeezed.

The fingers were like fiery bands of pain burning deep into my neck as they tightened slowly, slowly. I felt my face bulging, purpling with blood as my airway was ruthlessly blocked. My mouth gaped open in a vain struggle for air, my hands coming up to scrabble uselessly at her grip, tiny scraping noises breaking from my lips. My feet kicked and jerked involuntarily as the pressure increased. Something popped in my neck; the screaming agony as my windpipe gave way made my whole body convulse. A last, hollow whistle of pain escaped me and my hands fell away from hers. I realized, almost with relief, that I was dying. My vision of Zella's smiling face dimmed into silvery, darting swirls and then into nothingness.

Then there was light – unspeakable, glorious light. It closed over me and brought me up again from the shadows where I had fallen. Runnels of consciousness streamed out of me like water from an overfilled cup, and I seemed to dissolve into nothing and expand endlessly in the same moment. I became the light, was absorbed into it, existing wherever it coalesced. I was the great shining mantle of sky and clouds, the singing of the wind. I was the humming of stone and the unfurling whisper of green things, the laughter of water. I was the blood thrumming in every vein. I cried out with birthing infants and sighed the last breaths of the dying as I swept across the land in a great, never-ending flow of tides.

Memories flooded my mind: the memories of every wise woman who had ever lived. They all existed here, ageless, caught in the instant of their greatest power, when they had accepted this, had given into this.

All except my mother. My poor mother, who had died – had let Zella kill her – rather than face this terror, this wonder. Rather than face herself. Who had been so terrified that she had kept all knowledge of this from me and in doing so had unwittingly deprived me of the powers that should have been my birthright. At long last I understood Angharad's words, understood what my mother had kept from me. It had been within me all the time. In that pinpoint flash of excruciating clarity – the moment of death – I was everything, understood everything. I was the fulcrum upon which power turned. I was the heart of the land.

I looked into the body of the enaid – into my body – and saw the darkness that had infected it. Zella was a blot of rotted energy, a wound which had never healed properly. All her acts were like infection festered beneath the surface of the skin, leaving a trail of scar tissue in her wake. Gabriel's poor, swelling brain, my own crushed throat...

I let the swirling of the tides carry me to the source of the infection. I flowed into the darkness, into the oozing sore of hatred and anger and black enchantment and washed it clean. I felt the shadows stream up out of me, out of Zella – out of the world – into the light and disappear like smoke. And then there were no more shadows, no darkness, only the glowing light and rushing music of the tides.

The next instant – it all lasted no more than a second – I was back in my body again, dropping heavily to my knees, gasping for breath as Zella released me. My head spun from lack of oxygen and the suddenness of the transition as I looked up.

Zella cringed back from me, her face blanched with shock and pain. Then, with a howl of rage, she dropped onto all fours. Her skin burst open into flurries of red fur, body twisting and snapping into the shape of a creature like a wolf, but too large, with a body too low to the ground and a jaw too heavy, to be any ordinary wolf. It was only there for a moment before it began to change again, heaving and folding in on itself until it was much smaller, the livid chestnut fur sinking away into a silvery-grey pelt, the heavy bone-crushing jaw replaced by a sharp muzzle. A minute later I was looking at nothing more than a small grey fox. Then the fox was gone, melting into something human.

It was a girl not much older than I, her face worn into lines of care and sorrow. She had something of the look of Zella about her: a tiny woman, with long chestnut hair. But her eyes were brown, not black, and they welled up with moisture as she looked at me.

"Thank you," she said, a tear sliding slowly down her cheek.

"Be free, Mairid," I whispered.

The woman closed her eyes. The tear fell, a glitter of falling water, golden in the sun, and then there was nothing left of her but a small pile of river stones, worn smooth by the water and still shiny wet.

CHAPTER
EIGHTEEN

I felt moisture on my face and reached up with shaking fingers to touch it. I was crying, my heart and head too dazed to comprehend what had happened. My hand travelled down to my throat. It wasn't even bruised. But I winced as I tried to bend my little finger. It seemed my other injuries were unaffected.

There was silence in the courtyard. I glanced around to see everyone slumped together against the walls where they had sheltered, asleep. As I watched, they began to stir.

Gabriel.

I looked down and touched his face gently, but only to reassure myself; for there was no doubt he was breathing normally, his face a healthy colour again. Zella's work had been undone in time.

He opened his eyes at my touch, blinked twice, frowned, and sat up. "What—?"

I put a finger to his lips. "Time enough later. Hush now," I said.

"But... How?"

I left him sputtering and struggling to get up as I climbed to my feet. Every muscle in my body groaned and most of my bones clicked. I was fairly certain I had several cracked ribs, I knew my finger was broken, and my poor tooth needed urgent attention, but before I woke Rose and asked her to fix me, I needed to fix something myself.

Slowly, painfully, I lifted my arms. "Robin. David. Hugh." I whispered their names softly, reaching out for them with my mind.

They materialized slowly, a drifting cloud of silver whiteness that gently caressed my face and hair. Things that could have been feathers or stars or tiny white flowers fell around me like snow. I heard their voices in my head.

We love you

We forgive you -

We'll always be with you.

They thought I had called them to apologize for my failure in the working to restore them. Well, I had called them to apologize, but not for that.

"My darlings, I did this to you," I said. "It was me."

They were silent for a shocked moment. Then their voices burst into in my mind.

What? No! -
How can that be?
What do you mean?

"I'm so, so sorry." I whispered, torn between laughter and tears. "When Zella caught you, she tried to kill you. She was using spells far beyond anything Mother had taught me, and I didn't know how to fight them. I just reached out to try and protect you, in any way that I could; but I didn't know my own gift or my own strength. I pushed you away, out of range of her spells – I saved you, but I trapped you at the same time. I had no idea what I had done. I didn't even know I had the power to do such a thing. It was Great magic. In the normal way of things I could never have done it at all. But if I hadn't, then you would all have died."

But, but, but...

"I'm sorry! All my tunic-knitting was a waste of time." I scrubbed my face wearily with my battered fingers. "Angharad told me what to do, but I didn't understand. Robin, David, Hugh – this means you don't have to be swans any more. Now that I know what I did, I know how to set it right."

You do?

"You do?" Robin stared down at himself in disbelief. I was quite proud that I'd managed to bring him back in the same clothes he'd been wearing on the night I changed him.

"I ... I'm..." He burst into tears, falling to his knees. I

went down beside him and wrapped my arms around his heaving shoulders. A moment later, Hugh and David joined us, burying their faces in my hair as they sobbed.

"Oh, I missed you," I whispered, my voice breaking as I carefully embraced each of them. "I missed you, I missed you, so much."

I kneeled with them for several minutes, listening to their babbled threats to kill me and their deepest thanks. I touched Robin's red hair, and cupped David's stubborn jaw, and stared into Hugh's summer-blue eyes in awe and gratitude. For a long and terrible time I had thought I would never see them again. Now I could hardly believe that they were really here – that I had saved them after all.

After a while there was a gentle tap on my shoulder, and my brothers parted to let a crowd of other people in. Rose and the prince, and everyone else in the court-yard, had awoken. They wanted to be sure I was well, and find out what had happened. And who were these strange young men? And thank you – very much – for getting rid of whoever that woman had been. Several of them were holding river-smoothed pebbles wonder-ingly in their hands.

We had to tell them everything. Who our parents had been, and who we were, what had happened to us and how we had ended up here. The only part I couldn't tell them was how I had defeated Zella. Words, mun-dane, hollow words that a mouth could speak, were not designed to express something which only the soul could experience. So I didn't try.

Finally – thankfully, as by then I was so exhausted and weary I could hardly string two words together – Rose put a stop to the storytelling.

"Enough, now. Alexandra is exhausted, and none of us are fit for standing around," she said firmly. "I think we should all go inside and have the healers look at us."

At her direction David picked me up and carried me into the hall. Hugh and Rose between them helped Gabriel's grey-faced and rather subdued father along behind us. Gabriel, still shaky after his own encounter with Zella, was supported by Robin – but somewhere along the way he managed to find my hand, and clasped it carefully in his.

As our bedraggled group walked through the hall to the stairs, I smelled something intoxicating and sweet, and felt a dizzying sense of familiarity. I recognized the fragrance instantly. It was the scent I had smelled in my drugged sleep, so many months ago. It was the scent of roses.

I looked up, over my brothers' heads, at the ugly, thorny vine clinging stubbornly to the pierced stonework – and there, among the black leaves, I saw the golden gleam of new petals unfurling.

EPILOGUE

So we come to the end of my story. A year has passed since Zella attempted to invade Midland, and much has happened.

With the prince and princess of Midland's support, my brothers returned to the Kingdom and reclaimed it for David. We had worried there might be some resistance from Zella's court, but the majority of her supporters had already fled, and the others, returned to their senses now that she was gone, submitted without a whimper.

The rest has not been so easy. Our land is suffering a second year's crop failure, the long-term effect of the terrible drainage of its enaid, and of my own absence. I realize now that if only I had stayed in the Kingdom, Zella's task would have been impossible, for the life of the land would have had its heart to return to. Instead I was pouring my energy – unconsciously – into Midland. But I cannot regret the course of the past, not when I see the fields of Midland fertile and rich after so many years of barrenness. Gabriel and I hope that with all the help we can give, the Kingdom's people will survive, and the land recover.

Today the soil of the Kingdom is beneath my feet again. I have come home.

As I sit here in the long grasses by the river, I can see the damage which time has wrought to the place where I grew up. The once grand Hall has fallen into disrepair, the thatched roof caved in, the walls rotting, and all over-run with parasitic plants. Such houses are not built to survive neglect, and the Hall was forgotten when Zella persuaded my father to leave it; but David is determined to rule from this place as his Ancestors did, not from the half-built stone monstrosity which Zella squandered so much gold to build. Somewhere inside the crumbling shell, my brothers – and Gabriel too, of course – are wandering around, making plans for its reconstruction. Gabriel is determined to see my former home restored before we return to Midland together. It will take a lot of work, and a lot of time. But we are in no hurry.

In the meantime, the court has made a small camp, over the brow of the hill. There Gabriel's parents wait for us. It is in the camp that my betrothal to Gabriel will become official tonight, witnessed by both our families, among the brightly coloured tents and snapping flags, the garlands of flowers and the rugs spread on the grass. It will be merry and chaotic, like a picnic party gone mad, and not civilized at all.

My mother would have loved it.

Mother's gardens, to my great sorrow, have not survived. The plants are all dead. I believe, with some foundation, that they may have been that woman's first target when she wanted to drain the power from the land. Replanting and restoring them to their rightful beauty will probably take longer than the rebuilding of the Hall itself, but it will all be worth it, for there cannot be Hall without a gardens.

From the border of the gardens I hear my name called, and when I turn, Robin and Gabriel are standing there together, waiting for me. I look fondly at Robin's face, his eyes scrunched against the sunlight as he scans the field, calling for me again. But my gaze turns – as always – to Gabriel, who stands beside him. His hair is tousled into untidy ripples by the rising wind, and even from where I sit, I can see how the afternoon light makes his freckles glow.

Getting to my feet, I brush the dry leaves from my crumpled skirts and walk back to them through the waving grasses and wild flowers. When I reach them, I go up on tiptoe to kiss Gabriel and he tucks a curl of my hair back, and takes my hand in his. Robin smiles and rolls his eyes at us.

I pause for a moment and look back. From where I stand I can see the soft amber fronds of the meadows where I played as a child, and the shadow-green river with grass seeds and fallen leaves drifting on its surface like flakes of gold. I see the gentle rise of the hills beyond, marked by fields and forests. And I can see the enaid, skating through the clouds and on the wind, shining in the green things and shimmering in the water. I hear its susurration in the rustle of leaves and grasses, and taste it in the sweetness of the air.

A smile curves my lips. In the end, I know all will be well.

ACKNOWLEDGEMENTS

Writing a book is sometimes hard, but it's a piece of cake compared with trying to thank everyone who has helped you along the way. Nothing I say can ever express my love and gratitude to those people, but – I would like to thank:

Emil Fortune, editor, pal and all-round heck of a guy, without whom this book would never have been finished, let alone published. Yasmin Standen, for believing in me and this book, and always managing to say the right things. Hilary Van Dusen for taking on *The Swan Kingdom* for Candlewick Press, and being an utter delight to work with. Consider this the written equivalent of a big hug and kiss to all of you.

Georgie, the fabled Best Copy-Editor in the World, who made it fairly painless to see my manuscript covered in red scribbling. Steve Rawlings for cover art that literally made me cry with happiness, and Jim Bunker for wonderful ideas and beautiful hand lettering. All the rest of Walker Books whom I have met, for making me feel welcome at my first sales presentation, and kindly ignoring my tendency to babble hysterically.

The Furtive Scribblers: Barbara MG, Leah S, Holly, Susan Ang, Dr Tina Rath, and Rachel/Roccie. You are amazing people and I don't know what I would do without you. Come the glorious day, the cakes will be on me, I promise.

Rachel Penszor, Nic Robinson, Louise Robinson and Helen Tilson for reminding me that I'm supposed to have a life beyond my laptop. Long live Pizza Night!

The Forumites of the Advanced Book Exchange for being a bunch of biblio-obsessed, wise-cracking nutjobs, just like me.

Sasha Drennan, because simple kindness is the most important and the most under-rated virtue in the world.

And most of all, thank you to my family, especially my parents David and Elaine Marriott, for putting up with me for more than twenty years. I love you.

Maerad is a slave in a desperate and unforgiving settlement, taken there as a child when her family is destroyed in war. She is unaware that she possesses a powerful gift, a gift that marks her as a member of the School of Pellinor. It is only when she is discovered by Cadvan, one of the great Bards of Lirigon, that her true heritage and extraordinary destiny unfolds. Now she and her teacher, Cadvan, must survive a punishing and uncertain journey through a time and place where the dark forces they battle with stem from the deepest recesses of otherworldly terror.

This compelling historical novel tells of the love of two young people, in a society that forbids their being together. Susanna Thorn is a Quaker in Restoration England, and Will Heywood a rich country gentleman, captivated and intrigued by this plain-living, independent young woman. Conjuring up all the fear, prejudice and superstition of this century of great change and upheaval, including Civil War and Plague, this beautifully written tale will capture the imaginations of readers of all ages.